Trenton's Smile Knocked Away What Little Equilibrium Melodie Had Left.

When his arm suddenly blocked her path, her heart stopped. Then, when she looked up at him, so close to her, it started beating again. Too fast.

In one of those moments usually reserved for the movies, she just stood there, immobilized, staring into his eyes. She waited, expectantly, as he lowered his mouth to hers and claimed her lips in a possessive kiss.

He was always so stodgy, she had been sure he would be as methodical about kissing as he was about the rest of his life.

But oh, no. Here was where the soul of Trenton James Laroquette lived. His lips on hers were an invitation to joy, and his tongue was a gentle, coaxing summons to experience the decadently sensual.

And the summons was so tempting, so irresistible, it scared her to death....

Dear Reader,

The holidays are always a busy time of year, and this year is no exception! Our "banquet table" is chock-full of delectable stories by some of your favorite authors.

November is a time to come home again—and come back to the miniseries you love. Dixie Browning continues her TALL, DARK AND HANDSOME series with *Stryker's Wife*, which is Dixie's 60th book! This MAN OF THE MONTH is a reluctant bachelor you won't be able to resist! Fall in love with a footloose cowboy in *Cowboy Pride*, book five of Anne McAllister's CODE OF THE WEST series. Be enthralled by *Abbie and the Cowboy*—the conclusion to the THREE WEDDINGS AND A GIFT miniseries by Cathie Linz.

And what would the season be without HOLIDAY HONEYMOONS? You won't want to miss the second book in this cross-line continuity series by reader favorites Merline Lovelace and Carole Buck. This month, it's a delightful wedding mix-up with *Wrong Bride, Right Groom* by Merline Lovelace.

And that's not all! *In Roared Flint* is a secret baby tale by RITA Award winner Jan Hudson. And Pamela Ingrahm has created an adorable opposites-attract story in *The Bride Wore Tie-Dye*.

So, grab a book and give *yourself* a treat in the middle of all the holiday rushing. You'll be glad you did.

Happy reading!

Lucia Macro

Senior Editor
and the editors of Silhouette Desire

Please address questions and book requests to:
Silhouette Reader Service
U.S.: 3010 Walden Ave., P.O. Box 1325, Buffalo, NY 14269
Canadian: P.O. Box 609, Fort Erie, Ont. L2A 5X3

PAMELA INGRAHM
THE BRIDE WORE TIE-DYE

SILHOUETTE *Desire*®
Published by Silhouette Books
America's Publisher of Contemporary Romance

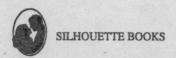 SILHOUETTE BOOKS

ISBN 0-373-76038-8

THE BRIDE WORE TIE-DYE

Books by Pamela Ingrahm

Silhouette Desire

Cowboy Homecoming #964
The Bride Wore Tie-Dye #1038

PAMELA INGRAHM

is a native Texan, filled with true Texas pride. She lives in Austin, and is still madly in love with her high school sweetheart. She also says her two children are the greatest kids in the world. Her experiences in over fourteen years as a legal assistant provide just some of her story ideas, and being an accomplished seamstress and quilter take up her "spare" time. "Becoming a published author is a dream come true," Pamela says, and she plans to keep dreaming for a long, long time.

To my children, the two greatest kids in the world: April and Mitchell. I love you both very much.

To Barbara: For all your support during the years before I "made it." You've been the greatest boss anybody could ever have.

To John, Susan and Diane: Thanks!

One

"**M**iss Melodie?"

Melodie Allford whirled in surprise at the deep, decidedly masculine tone. On any given day, she heard her name called a hundred times, but the chorus of voices was usually several octaves higher. In fact, the chorus had just gone squealing to the four-through-six-year-old's playground at Little Angels Day Care, leaving her—and the beginnings of a whopper headache—in blessed quiet to finish stacking the mats.

She took one look at the body that belonged to this voice and decided that yes, Virginia, there was a Santa Claus, and he had been very, very good to this man.

She suppressed a wry grin and decided there was just enough small-town girl in her to be a little dazzled by what she saw. She clutched the tumbling mat to her like a lifeline.

She rarely met the parents of the children she taught dance to, as her classes were over well before pick-up time. This, however, was one father she truly regretted not getting to meet sooner.

He was tall—easily six-three or six-four. Mmm... perfect. At five foot nine, she was hardly a giant, but she liked looking up at her dance partners.

He also had black hair with just a whisper of gray starting to show at his temples. Very distinguished.

And blue eyes. Deep, dark blue, fringed by thick, black lashes. Lashes that most women would kill for. Dark brows that arched like guardians.

Tanned. Not a dark tanning-bed tan, but a warm, I-get-out-in-the-sun tan that his crisp white shirt showed off to perfection.

And what a body! For all that his perfectly proper navy suit probably had a Brooks Brothers or Joseph Banks or heaven only knew what other label in it—which she could forgive this once—the body in the suit was great. It included broad shoulders, a narrow waist and legs she would pay good money to see in a pair of cutoffs. Or better yet, biker's shorts. In fact, she wondered just what he did to look so mouth-wateringly good. Jog? Swim?

Melodie couldn't wait until he left so she could check out the rear view.

On second thought, yes, she could. She could stand here and watch him for the next hour. If he'd oblige.

She wondered if his wife appreciated just what she had. Then again—she straightened a little—where was it written he was married? There were lots of single dads out there these days....

When she realized she had yet to speak to the man, she felt that dratted blush creep up her neck. No doubt, next to her red hair, her usually paler-than-a-bedsheet complexion now looked like an anemic sunburn—as it did any time she got flustered.

"Um, yes, I'm Melodie Allford. Can I help you?"

There. That sounded casual, businesslike and refined. Nothing to reveal her still-erratic pulse.

As if her belated greeting were his cue, he took a step closer and held out his hand. "I'm Trenton Laroquette. Amber Dawson's uncle."

Ah, yes. Trenton James Laroquette, Esquire, to be precise. Or so his letterhead had read. Then the man smiled. And Melodie's knees melted.

"It's a pleasure to meet you," she said, surprised at how flustered she felt by a mere handshake.

Hope sprang eternal in her young heart. Uncle, not dad. No wedding ring, although that was no guarantee. Charming, urbane, handsome.

Hope strangled itself when she realized how she was dressed. Her outfit of white leggings embroidered with pigs, black jogging shorts and a purple tie-dyed shirt was a little wild, even by her own standards. If she dared move the tumbling mat which, for the moment, was an effective shield, she had the sinking feeling Mr. Wonderful would become Mr. Displeased. Somehow she doubted that a guy who looked as if he'd stepped off the cover of *GQ* would understand how well children responded to outfits such as this. After all, this *was* a creative dance class....

In fact, the more she thought about it, the more mournful hope's sigh became. This guy was all Wall Street and black lacquer desks—or whatever passed for uptight-corporate-mogul in Austin, Texas, these days. She doubted he'd have much tolerance for a single thirty-something who spent her days teaching improv dance to little kids and her nights deciding between chicken noodle or vegetable beef. On an exciting evening, she added oyster crackers.

"The pleasure is mine, Miss Allford. I'm sorry for my informal address when I arrived, but Amber only calls you Miss Melodie. Could I inquire if you've received my letter?"

Could he inquire? Melodie felt hope give one last kick as it turned up its toes and fell into the grave. She wished he had let her keep her illusions just a bit longer before confirming he was completely uptight. He was probably going to pick a wife who wore little lace collars and blushed demurely at every turn. Not that Melodie was one to cast stones. She blushed all the time—the common curse of a redhead—but never demurely.

"Peanut butter and all," she said, almost laughing at his confused expression. She decided she'd better cut out the wisecracks. Too many jokes might confuse the poor man. "Your concept for a children's workout video is interesting, and the role of instructor sounds intriguing, but..."

Her voice faded and her eyes widened when he shrugged out of his jacket and slung it over his shoulder, hooked on one finger. She'd seen it in the movies and thought the move was incredibly sexy. Without a doubt, it was more potent in person.

"Trenton!"

A voice boomed from behind the tall man. Melodie had never been so glad to see Serena, the owner of the day-care center, as she was right now. Serena's entrance had beautifully covered her momentary gape-mouthed loss for words.

"Good afternoon, Serena. How has your day been?"

"Busy. I see you've met Melodie," she said, gesturing with the antenna of the walkie-talkie that was so much a part of her. Melodie thought Serena probably felt naked without it.

"Yes, we were just talking about the video," Trenton said, casting a polite glance to both women.

We were? Melodie kept her expression carefully neutral.

Serena smiled, obviously glad one task was off her hands. "Great! I've got to stop by the baby room, but then I'll head back to the playground and get T-1 and T-2 ready to go for you."

When they were alone again, Trenton spoke first. "Could I assist you with these mats?"

"No! Um, I—I mean, thank you," she stuttered, covering her reaction and clutching the mat even tighter. "It won't take me a minute to finish."

"Uncle Trenton!"

The squeal could belong to no one but Amber. She barreled by Melodie, knocking the mat out of her hands and sending it crashing to the floor.

Joey came to a skidding halt behind his younger sister. "Hey, Uncle Trenton." He glanced at the mat as if wondering whether he should pick it up.

Trenton bent for it at the same time Melodie did, and they knocked foreheads. They both raised fingers to their now-tender temples as Serena came hurrying up behind them. Her hand unit began hissing static, adding to the chaos.

"Serena? This is Ginger. Amber and Joey saw their uncle's car and took off like jackrabbits. Are they up there?"

Serena keyed her walkie-talkie. "We got 'em, Ginger. Don't leave your class. They're fine."

"Tell those two rapscallions we're going to have a little talk tomorrow."

"Ten-four."

Amber ducked her head and looked at her uncle from beneath her lashes. With her arms behind her back, she said, "I'm sorry, Uncle Trenton."

Melodie took the moment to retrieve the mat and place it on the stack against the wall. The damage was done so there was no sense hiding any longer. As she walked back to the center of the room, she watched Trenton bend down on one knee and chuck the little girl under the chin.

"Don't tell me you're sorry, you little imp. Tell Miss Ginger."

"I will. 'Morrow."

"*To*morrow, then." He turned to Joey. "And you, young man—"

Joey's expression fell. "I'm sorry, too."

He pulled the boy into a short, fierce hug. "This is hardly the end of the world, guys. It's only that the school is so big, you can't just go running off."

"I know, Uncle Trenton. I'll apologize after Amber."

"Good enough. Now, who wants to go with me to Kidstravaganza?"

Melodie rolled her eyes, thinking he might as well have asked who wanted to meet Mickey Mouse. Amber and Joey went into hyperactive mode, jumping and screaming enough to hurt her ears.

Amber suddenly stopped and turned her head from Uncle Trenton to Melodie and back again. "Can Miss Melodie go?"

"Oh, no, honey—" Melodie tried to break in.

"Pleeaase, Uncle Trenton?"

"Honey, I can't—"

"She read your letter and told me she was gonna call you about the video. You could talk while Joey and I play," Amber suggested innocently, her eyes as wide as she could make them.

Trenton looked at her and Melodie felt her breath catch.

"Miss Allford?"

"Melodie, please. And really, I can't. I'm hardly dressed—"

He arched an eyebrow, once again taking in her leggings—pigs and all. "Oh, I think you'd be right at home."

Darn, and she thought he might not have noticed her attire in the momentary confusion. But as she thought about it, it was her turn to arch a brow. She perceived a challenge in his voice. She could always plead that she had a class to teach, but it would be a lie. And she never lied. She might not always volunteer the whole story, but she never lied.

"Be that as it may, I'm not—"

"Pleeaase, Miss Melodie. Please go with us. It'll be tons of fun. Please say you'll go."

If she hadn't looked into Amber's eyes, she might have held her ground, but Melodie rarely stood a chance against a child's plea or a puppy's whine. Which was why she avoided pet shops at all costs....

"Oh, all right."

She knew the effort to have a meeting would be futile. An indoor playground was hardly conducive to business discussions, but she decided Amber's hug would make the wasted afternoon worthwhile.

"You know Terminator-1, don't you, Miss All-ford?" Trenton asked, ruffling Joey's hair.

Joey shied out from under the offending hand, try-ing not to show he liked the gesture.

"And I'm T-2," Amber piped up, grinning from ear to ear.

Melodie smiled. "Yes, Joey and I have met, and we get along pretty well. Even if he does think dance is for sissies."

"Really, Joey? I like to dance."

"That's not the same, Uncle Trenton. You do real dancing."

Trent chuckled as he slipped his suit jacket back on, snapping the lapels neatly into place. "I have a feel-ing that postadolescence will alter your conviction on the subject, but for now, let's go. We don't want to take any chances on them running out of pizza."

Melodie felt another heart tug as Trenton hefted T-2 into his arms. She realized she was holding her breath, waiting for him to scold Amber for wrinkling his suit, and was pleasantly surprised when he didn't even seem to notice. She glanced down to snap her hip pouch around her waist, thankful her ducked head would hide any revealing expression on her face.

Everyone said goodbye to Serena and moved to the parking lot. A wave of the late June heat rolled off the concrete and hit Melodie like a slap. She stopped in her tracks and heaved a disgusted sigh. She wiped at the sweat already forming on her forehead, betting her-self a nickel Mr. Perfect would never be so crass as to perspire in public.

"Hey, Trent. You know that old saying, 'It's not the heat, it's the humidity'?"

Trenton stopped as well, turning toward her. "Yes?"

"Baloney. It's the heat."

His laugh was another thing that took her by surprise. It was deep and mellow and wrapped comfortably around her like a soft blanket. She mentally shook her head. Scratch that simile. Make that a cool breeze.

"Would you like to go in one car? That is, if you can stand being in confined quarters with these two miniature whirlwinds."

She declined politely. "I think I'll follow. Thanks anyway." She felt no need to explain to him that one of her rules was to never allow herself to be dependent on another person.

"Do you know where the establishment is?"

"They're only running advertisements on the television every five minutes. Yes, I know where it is."

"Good. Shall we meet there in . . . say, twenty minutes?"

She had the absurd urge to affect an English accent and say, "Right ho, old boy." Instead, she said, "That sounds great."

He stopped again and looked at her. "Miss Allford—"

For heaven's sake, didn't the man know how to loosen up? They were going to a playground and he was acting as if she were his teacher instead of Amber's.

"Look, if you keep calling me Miss Allford, you're going to regret it."

A mocking smile played at the corner of his mouth. "That sounds vaguely threatening, Miss Allford."

"There's nothing vague about it at all, T.J."

Trenton winced. "I concede the point. Melodie."

She smiled as she turned, shrugging a shoulder at him. "Good. See you in a few."

Melodie opened the door to her aging compact and let some of the blisteringly hot air dissipate. Not that it mattered much. Without air-conditioning, the car was always on the wrong side of miserable from June until October. But no use complaining about it. A new car was just going to have to wait until she paid off the new air conditioner she'd bought for the house, figuring driving in the heat was preferable to sleeping in it.

She felt a moment of envy as Trenton and the kids flashed by in a dark blue luxury car, windows rolled up tightly. Then she reminded herself that if the price of owning a nice vehicle was being like Mr. Stodgy, she didn't want to pay it.

Of course, it was easier to be smug in December....

As they headed out of the parking lot, Melodie pushed away a fleeting wish that she could have changed into something a little less dramatic. But that was water under the bridge. Better to make the best of it and get this over with.

Two

Trenton nodded as the quartet claimed a table in one of the large eating rooms. It appeared they had arrived at a most propitious time. The majority of the day-care groups were leaving, and the after-work crowd had yet to arrive as it was only four o'clock.

The ambiance was exactly as he had expected, which pleased Trenton. He didn't like surprises.

Behind sound-reducing sheets of clear Plexiglas, parents and other nonparticipants could watch the fun being had on the giant plastic activity centers, each one a different, brilliant primary color.

What made Kidstravaganza unique was its policy of encouraging parents to play with their kids. Of the three sections, only one was designated exclusively for children. The other two were built on a larger scale—still inviting to small folk, but with tubes and entries large enough for an adult to join in.

Amber and Joey were almost beside themselves to go into the play area. Miss Allford...um, Melodie...looked decidedly less enthusiastic than the children, but he sensed mixed signals from her. He could swear that she would love to dive into the vat of plastic balls right behind the first child, so he assumed it was his presence that had her twisting the hem of her tie-dyed T-shirt with a purple-tinted fingernail. He noted absently that the ring finger of her left hand was bare, but he knew in this day and time that didn't mean much.

He assured himself that his perusal for a wedding band was simply habit, for although Melodie was a beautiful woman, she was a little more...flamboyant than he was used to. He was still surprised at the evolution of his reactions to women over the past year. His criteria had changed into something quite different than when he'd been merely dating. Now that he was almost forty, he was looking for more than a fun evening with a woman. He wanted to find that special someone to love and build a family with.

He noticed that habits barely recognized before bothered him now. For instance, when a woman wore too much perfume. He decided that would upset a baby. Or when someone was too thin. The mother of his children had to be health-conscious, not consumed by dress size. In fact, one of his recent patterns was to take his prospective candidates to functions where children would be present to see how they reacted. He wasn't vain, but neither was he coy— he knew that in the dating game all parties tended to put on their best fronts and he didn't want to waste precious time with someone who claimed she loved kids, when in fact, she didn't.

Looking at Joey and Amber, he knew one thing for certain: he wanted a couple of towheaded imps running around his house, causing general chaos and filling his life the way these two did his sister's. He had stepped in and helped Bridgette these past few years, but the fact remained that although Amber and Joey loved him, he was only their uncle, not their dad.

Now that Bridgette had reclaimed her confidence and joy, he was sure she wouldn't stay in Austin forever. He expected an engagement announcement from her and Glen any day, especially with Glen making noises about moving with his job. Trenton liked the guy, and it didn't hurt that Glen adored Bridgette and doted on Joey and Amber.

He glanced at Melodie and wondered how she felt about kids. He had every reason to guess she adored them or she would hardly have picked teaching them as a profession. But, then, he knew appearances could be deceiving. She might just as easily be locked into a job she hated because she didn't have any other options. Millions of people went to work every day fitting that description. Watching her, though, he didn't think she was one of them. She looked at Amber with too much tenderness, and her fingers were so gentle when she brushed his niece's overlong bangs out of her face. Even with Joey, who had so indelicately insulted dancing as a whole, Melodie seemed amused.

It spoke well of her, but only added to his confusion. His picture so far was incongruous. He assumed that would change when they got a chance to talk. She had such a delicate face, her eyes a haunting mixture of caution and joy, as if she wanted to greet life with open arms but had been taught to keep her hands carefully at her sides. She was a soft touch with the kids, but she looked at him now and again with a hard reserve, as if preparing to do battle. If he'd seen a picture of her from the neck up, he would have expected to find her in a soft, flowing dress that dipped in front in a delicate heart shape. Instead, she appeared in leggings that had pigs embroidered on them.

Pigs!

But those pigs marched down an incredible set of legs. They clung to thighs and calves that were long and sleek, with muscles that were toned and taut.

Made a man think he just might not mind being a pig.

And the T-shirt would have been painful to look at for long stretches, except that the material was soft and lay against her feminine curves in a gentle caress. It might be loose fitting, but he was confident it hid firm, high breasts that begged to be kissed. Her nipples would be rosy and would harden instantly when his tongue—

Trenton shook his head. Good heavens, what had gotten into him? It took an effort to pull his thoughts back on track and remind himself that although his first impressions were favorable, she was not an appropriate candidate for consideration as a future wife so he could stop the preliminary interview that instant.

Besides, he had the distinct impression that Melodie Allford defied categorization.

"Can we go now?"

Amber was dancing from foot to foot. She had dutifully removed her shoes and glanced longingly into the play area. Joey stood just as eagerly at her side.

He smiled indulgently. "Sure. You guys go ahead."

Amber stopped in her tracks. "Aren't you going in with us?"

"Not right now. I need to talk to Miss Melodie, remember?"

"You got plenny a time. Come on, Uncle Trenton. You promersed."

Trenton looked at Melodie, giving her the chance to put in her two cents' worth. She smiled wryly and shook her head, obviously seeing the uselessness of arguing.

"Maybe after pizza we can send them off alone," Trenton suggested.

"One could always hope."

He wasn't quite sure what she meant by that, but Amber and Joey weren't giving him time to dwell on it. Joey stuffed his shoes into a cubby before bringing a basket to the table for keys, loose change, cuff links and cellular phone. Amber was determinedly making a knot out of Trenton's shoelace as she tried to "help," but he didn't have the heart to stop her just yet.

A look in Melodie's direction as he rolled back his sleeves had him noting that she was still standing by the viewing window, but she was looking at him as though he were an experiment under glass. She kept glancing at his bare forearms, then his socks, then back at his face as if she couldn't put a picture together.

"Aren't you forgetting something?" he asked to break her concentration, glancing pointedly at her athletic shoes and then at her hip pouch.

She started. "Me? Oh, no, I'm not—"

"Come on, Miss Melodie," Amber said, abandoning her uncle to run over and grab Melodie's hand. "You gotta come with us or it won't be no fun."

"Any fun."

"Right," Amber agreed, the soul of reasonableness.

Trenton had finished the job Amber had begun and had moved over to her side. "You might as well give in. You know you can't win."

With an exaggerated sigh, Melodie put her hipsack in the locker and took the rear of the short line headed toward the nautical area. The "gangplank" led to a series of jungle gyms designed as ships. The ball bin had been done in blues and greens, and the climbing vines were thick, knotted ropes.

"Argh, maties, and welcome aboard," an eye-patched attendant greeted them out of the side of his mouth as they stepped onto the deck. "I'll be remindin' ye to have fun, but be careful. The high seas are no place for high jinks, ya' know."

Melodie felt a tug at the hem of her shorts. "What are high gins?" Amber asked in a loud whisper.

The attendant went down on one knee and motioned Amber closer. Cautiously, Amber inched forward.

"High jinks, me wee lass, are things such as pushin' and shovin' while yer playin', and running pell-mell without watchin' where yer goin'."

"Oh, we won't do that," Amber promised solemnly, shaking her head.

"All righty then, that's a good lass. Now hurry aboard so's I can get the lines cast off and we can set sail."

* * *

Melodie didn't know when she'd had so much fun. Or been so confused.

She laughed herself silly when Amber and Joey engaged in a "water" fight with their uncle, showering him with brightly colored balls until he was buried to the neck. She clapped dutifully when Amber cried, "Watch me, watch me," as she "walked the plank" and "splashed" into the "ocean." Joey climbed the "rigging" like a monkey, taunting his Uncle Trenton to catch him if he could. Of course, Uncle Trenton gave a valiant effort, but was no match for the agile seaman Joey.

She felt the oddest tug in her stomach when Amber decreed that they were a family taken captive by awful pirates and were going to make a desperate escape through the "hold" of the ship. Amber bravely led the way through the plastic tunnels, twisting and turning through the maze. Melodie had a hard time keeping her mind on the game with Trent right behind her. She sighed when they finally reached the "escape hatch" and the foursome slid down the long slide one by one to end up in the "ocean" again.

The successful escapees finally returned to the "dock." The adults slid into their chairs, and worked at restoring their breathing to normal. Melodie wanted to frown when she noticed that maybe it was just her who was out of breath, and she was in pretty good shape. Trenton was already fixing his cuffs and slipping his jacket back on. She tried to deny it, but she was disappointed. The afternoon had been fun. She didn't want Trenton to return to being *Perfect Man— Defender of Decorum, Protector of Protocol.*

The miniature pirates, legs swinging wildly, began chanting, "Pizza! Pizza!"

The magic words brought a waitress to their sides.

"Good afternoon, and welcome to Kidstravaganza. My name is Veronica and I'll be your hostess."

Melodie was of the uncharitable opinion that Veronica's too-sweet smile just might put her in a sugar coma. The thought was immediately followed by a frown. She was rarely catty, so she couldn't figure out what had made her react that way. It surely couldn't be the admiring glances being cast in Trenton's direction. Admittedly, he looked incredibly attractive in his disheveled state, but even if Veronica was flirting with him, what did that matter to Melodie?

It didn't matter at all, as a matter of fact. If Veronica the bimbo wanted to play goo-goo eyes with Trenton, then she could just knock herself out. Melodie refused to make a fool of herself for any man, especially one as unattainable as this rich lawyer guy. If she was on the hunt, which she most certainly was not, she knew better than to pick someone so completely opposite from her type. And Mr. Perfectly-Pressed-Suit-and-Tie was definitely *not* her style.

Before she realized it, pizza and salad had been ordered without her input and Veronica was sashaying away.

"—hope that's all right."

"What?" she asked, trying to focus on Trenton's words.

"I said, you didn't say anything while I was ordering so I hope pepperoni pizza and a pitcher of cola is all right with you."

"Yes, that's fine. I would rather have had iced tea but that's okay."

His forehead furrowed. "I'm sorry. I'll call her back—"

"No. That's okay. It's not worth the hassle."

"Yes, it is, if that's what you want. I should have gotten your attention sooner."

A headache was building behind her right eye. "I said it was all right. We're talking about a glass of tea here, not a new car."

"Melodie—"

"For heaven's sake! Does anyone ever argue with you?" she snapped as she pressed two fingers against her closed eye.

He was obviously taken aback.

"That's what I thought. Look, Trenton the Valiant, if I was determined to have the stupid drink, I'd let you come to my rescue and reorder. So can we just drop it?"

"Certainly."

A glance across the table told her she'd just insulted the man again.

She sighed. "I apologize. That was unfair. I know you don't know me very well, but I'm not usually this grumpy." In the time it had taken her to argue with him, the pain in her head had gone from a twinge to near agony.

He must have heard the sincerity in her voice for his body language changed immediately. "Please don't give it another thought. I can see you're not feeling well."

"Are you all right, Miss Melodie?"

Melodie forced a smile for Amber's sake. "I'm fine, sweetheart. My head just hurts a little bit."

"Do you have a sperin?"

Trenton looked at Amber, frowning. "A what?"

"An aspirin," Melodie supplied. "I have some medicine in my glove compartment. I'll go get it in a minute."

"I'll collect it for you," Trenton said as he stood. Joey had given him the key, and they had the locker open before Melodie could protest.

"It's all right, really. I'll go out in a minute."

She had no intention of telling him she'd rather endure her headache than have him get a close-up look of her car. Right behind that thought came the taunt of: why should she care what he thought of her car? And on the heels of that came the brilliant final thrust of: she just did, that's why.

Her protest proved unsurprisingly futile as she watched Trent leave the building. The children were quiet, their little faces serious.

She smiled again. "Hey, guys, I'm fine. Don't look so glum. It's just a little headache."

The reassurance didn't work. She didn't get them to smile at her until Trent handed her the bottle of medicine and she swallowed a pill.

"See, all better."

Freed from their concern, the kids dug into the newly arrived pizza. Melodie tried, but it would be a while yet before she could eat. More unnerving than the headache—which would dissipate as soon as the medicine hit her system—were Trent's assessing glances over the table.

"Please don't be concerned. I get these all the time. I'm feeling much better." She couldn't explain why she felt the urge to reassure him.

"I'm glad." He looked at her again, his expression unfathomable. "You, Miss Allford, are a mass of incongruity."

Surprise set her back in her chair. "What makes you say that, Mr. Laroquette?"

"I can't read you very well, and that bothers me."

"So is this a crime punishable by jail time, or merely a fine?" A smile tugged at the corner of her mouth.

"No crime, just a surprise."

"Oh, good. I like surprises."

He glanced at her sharply. "I don't."

"Really? Why?"

He studied her for a long moment but didn't answer. She felt compelled to cover the silence.

"I guess I'm probably your worst nightmare, then. I've been told by more than one person that I absolutely defy logic."

"I think that's a female prerogative."

"Oh! Already on to the sexist comments."

"No, just a statement of fact. And I didn't say it was a bad thing. It's what makes women such wonderfully complex, stimulating creatures."

Melodie knew she should be feeling the politically correct righteous anger that his statement ought to invoke, but somehow she knew that he meant it as a compliment. Her gut told her this man was a Southern gentleman. She'd bet her bottom dollar that he would treat any woman as his equal in the business world, but he still opened doors and held coats and walked dates to their doors. She personally felt there was room to be strong and still be feminine. The two were not mutually exclusive.

"I'm not the only incongruity around here," she shot back, breaking out of her reverie.

"Oh, yeah?"

"Yeah. You're quite an enigma yourself."

"So I guess we're both intrigued."

"Possibly, but I have to be honest and tell you that I feel you're being coerced into including me on this project."

"I—"

"Uncle Trenton, Joey's sticking his tongue out."

"Am not!"

"Are, too!"

"Hold it, guys," Trenton interjected before an all-out brawl ensued. "What's going on?"

Joey lowered his eyes to the table. "Nothing."

"Uh-huh," Amber argued. "He was bein' gross."

"Joey?" Trenton waited, a wealth of questions behind the simple name.

"I was just trying to be funny. She's just a little ninny, that's all."

Ninny? Melodie wondered. She had no idea kids used the word *ninny* these days.

"Are you guys finished eating?" The two nodded. "Then why don't you go play on the second playground."

The two were off like bolts of lightning, and Trenton shook his head. "I just love those kids."

"They are darlings, that's for sure. Can I make a big leap here and assume they are the reason behind this video?"

"Part of it, certainly. My market research gives me hope that it will also be a lucrative project. It would be a nice addition to their trust funds."

Melodie settled back and crossed her legs comfortably. "How did you get started in all this?"

"Their mother, who is my sister, is a radio/TV/film major at U.T. Bridgette has to do a video for a school assignment and she mentioned one day that she couldn't find any good children's exercise videos. We both just looked at each other."

Melodie raised an eyebrow. "And the rest, as they say, is history?"

"Pretty much. Her project doesn't have to be marketed, but after doing some research, we figured that if she was going to do all that work, she might as well get something out of it."

"Just she? You're not involved?"

"I'm fronting the expenses, but that's all I'm going to let Bridgette pay me back. This is for her and the kids."

"That's awfully nice of you."

"They're very special to me."

The love and caring she saw in his eyes made her uncomfortable. He was obviously the kind of big brother every girl dreamed of having. Bridgette was one of the lucky ones to actually get an older sibling like Trenton. Other big brothers weren't quite as close to the mark.

She cleared her throat. "So where do I come in?"

"We envision this as a dance video. We had someone lined up to lead it, but she had to back out due to an illness in her family. Now we need to recast the role."

After they briefly discussed the financial terms, Melodie admitted she was interested, but every time she looked at Trenton, her gut meter went off in warning. It was the voice that said, "Danger! Nice guy ahead." Nice guys, as a whole, were all right, but they tended to be awfully straitlaced.

Worse yet, she knew from some of Serena's gossip that Trent was not only a nice guy, he was a nice guy hunting for a wife. Not that he'd ever cast her in *that* role, but the last thing she needed was to be locked into a project with a guy that made her nervous. And nice guys could never understand that she wasn't going to sacrifice who she was on the altar of marriage. Men always started out saying they won't ask a woman to give up her career or her dreams, but she'd watched too many of her friends cave in when their husbands put on the pressure. She didn't have the time or the desire to play that game.

Time. Now there was the real problem. She didn't have the time to devote to this project, even if she were so inclined. So all in all, it would just be easiest if she let them both off the hook.

"Look, Trent, I appreciate you talking to me about the video and all, but I don't think I'm your girl."

He looked at her for a long moment, and Melodie appreciated his honesty by not offering false disappointment.

"If you're sure . . ." he began.

Melodie nodded. "Yes, I think it would be best. I do want to thank you for the opportunity."

"My pleasure."

She doubted it, but it was nice of him to say anyway.

They stood and were shaking hands when Joey burst into the room. "Uncle Trenton! Amber threw up!"

Trent turned and raced to the play area. He'd barely reached the door when Amber came through and launched herself into his arms, tears streaming down her face.

"I was just..." The rest of her words were lost in her sobs. Melodie stroked the child's head comfortingly.

"She was hanging upside down on the monkey bars when she hurled all over everything. It was cool!" Joey supplied with typical brotherly concern.

Attendants hurried to the area with cleaning supplies, and a manager came over to them. "Is the child all right, sir?"

"Yes, she's fine. I should have made her wait longer after eating."

"That's quite all right. This happens often."

Trenton stood with Amber in his arms and gave Melodie a wry smile over the little girl's shoulder. "Look, Melodie—"

They both gave exasperated sighs as his cellular phone chirped in his pocket. Shifting Amber, he answered the summons.

Feeling awkward about listening to his side of the conversation, Melodie tried to focus her attention elsewhere. This was one of those situations the protocol police needed to come up with some new rules for. Did one stand there and listen obviously? Did one look off and pretend not to listen? Did one physically move away? Melodie decided if she could find the time she was going to write a book: *Cellular Phones and the Men Who Love Them*.

It should be a bestseller.

Thankfully, he kept the conversation short. When she brought her attention back to him, it was obvious that he wasn't exactly happy.

"That was Bridgette."

Melodie waited, not sure that a response was required.

"I told her that you declined, but she insisted I invite you to dinner at my house tonight. We're having a meeting of the video staff at seven-thirty. It will be informal."

Melodie wanted to inquire which would be informal—the dinner or the meeting.

"Please, Miss Melodie," Amber said, her blue eyes liquid with tears. "I want you to meet my mommy."

"No, honey. Not this time. I promise you I'll stay after school one afternoon and meet her, okay?"

Barely mollified, Amber nodded and rested her head against her uncle's broad chest.

After giving Amber a final pat, Melodie smiled at Trent. "Thank you again, but no. I'll just go so you can take care of the kids."

Trenton held out his hand and shook hers warmly once more. "I appreciate your time, Melodie." He reached into his pocket for a pen. "Here's my card," he said as he wrote on the back, "in case you change your mind. It was nice talking with you."

"You, too. Goodbye."

In a blink, it seemed, they were outside and heading for their respective vehicles. As she slipped inside her traveling sauna, Melodie wondered how she'd gotten herself into another fine mess with so little effort. At least she had gotten herself out of it without any damage.

She was still lost in thought as she pulled into the driveway of her little cookie-cutter home. Her address might not be in Hyde Park or Tarrytown or any of the other wonderful neighborhoods she'd love to live in, but it was hers—and the bank's.

She wondered for a moment where Mr. Trenton James Laroquette, Esquire, lived. She could only imagine. Probably in the house of her dreams.

Well, wherever he lived, the fresh coat of paint she'd put on last year still looked good and other than the fact that the yard was overdue to be mowed, the place was neat and tidy.

The first thing she did after opening the door was flip on the air conditioner. It was one of the few luxuries she afforded herself, and her standing rule was to turn it on when she got home in the evening and leave it on until she left for work the next morning. It was a little stuffy now, but the house would be blessedly cool for the rest of the night.

As she headed through the living area toward the dining room, something nagged at the edges of her consciousness. It wasn't until she was almost done flipping through the stack of mail on the table that she realized what it was.

Things were missing.

The Led Zepelin poster was gone. Half the CD rack was gone. The gray recliner and end table were gone.

Most of all, she guessed her roommate was gone.

Three

Melodie glanced around and noticed a few more things missing. Danielle hadn't exactly been a neatnik, so the very fact that the place looked organized was surprising. Even Danielle's room was clean—simply void of any personal effects.

When Melodie reached her room, she headed straight for the shower, leaving a trail of sweaty clothes across the floor. She loosened her braid and ran her fingers through her long, heavy hair as she adjusted the water temperature and stepped under the spray. She planned on standing there until her fingers started to wrinkle.

She didn't quite make it to wrinkle stage before turning off the taps, but she did feel cool and refreshed. She wondered if it was odd to feel more from a shower than from a roommate who had abandoned her, leaving her in the lurch, but Melodie pushed the thought away as she wrapped one towel turban-style around her head and tucked another under her arms.

She supposed she should feel something—any-thing—since Danielle was gone, but the most she could come up with was a mild sense of relief mixed with an even milder twinge of disappointment. It wasn't as if she hadn't known this was coming.

Then she noticed an envelope propped against her pillow. In the enclosed note Danielle had said she'd "hooked up" with an old boyfriend and had to "split" all of a sudden. After ending the note with a hope that Melodie would be "cool" about all this, Danielle had signed off with "later."

Danielle's timing, as well as her writing style, left a lot to be desired.

This event certainly cast a new light on the video is-sue. She might actually need this job! If only she hadn't declined so quickly. Not that she believed she'd had much of a chance of earning the part, but she was now motivated to at least give it a shot.

She glanced at the clock. Trent had said they were getting together at seven-thirty, and it was just after six. If she called, she might be able to get herself rein-vited to the meeting.

In the time it took to retrieve his business card from her hip pack and return to the bedroom, her stomach had twisted into a knot. Her hand trembled as she punched out the numbers on the phone. Hesitating before hitting the last button, she slammed the re-ceiver back into its cradle. She didn't have to do this! She could always pick up a part-time job somewhere until the crisis was over. Besides, she'd just bet Tren-ton was a tightwad as well as a stuffed shirt and wouldn't want to pay her what she was worth.

Despite the fact that she was alone, Melodie felt her face flush. That thought was mean and unworthy of her. She didn't know why she was so dead set on believing the worst about Trenton Laroquette. She just couldn't put her finger on what it was about him that affected her so.

Taking a deep breath, she reached for the phone again, and this time, completed the call.

"'lo?" a childish voice answered.

"Amber? This is Miss Melodie. Is your uncle there?"

All Melodie heard was a squeal, a crash as the phone bounced off a table or desk and a shrill shriek of "Uncle Trenton, Uncle Trenton! Come quick! It's Miss Melodie!"

Melodie smiled and shook her head.

Her smile wavered when she heard Trent's voice. "Melodie?"

She cleared her throat. "I apologize for the surprise, but I was thinking about your offer and wondering if the invitation to the meeting tonight still held good."

There was a moment's hesitation—just enough to make her nervous.

"Yes, of course. You're quite welcome to join us."

She let out a silent sigh of relief. "Great. Um, it's at seven-thirty, right?"

"That's correct. Let me give you directions to my home."

She scrambled for a pen and turned Danielle's letter over for scratch paper, mentally berating herself for not being prepared. Maybe subconsciously she hadn't believed he would say yes.

Glancing at the clock as she hung up, she realized she would have to hurry to get ready and make it halfway across town in time.

But she also knew that, in a hurry or not, she needed to put her best foot forward. With quick strokes, she brushed her hair until it glowed. Pulling the sides back, she gave it a simple twist and used her favorite Chinese comb to hold it in place while the rest cascaded down her back. She chose a wrap skirt in a bright Southwest print and topped it with a turquoise-colored silk tank top. A gold necklace and big gold hoops in her ears were her only jewelry. She slipped tan sandals on her feet as she stuck her cheap but functioning watch into the purse she would use instead of her too-casual hip pack.

Always a minimalist with makeup, she found herself applying what little she did wear with care. She needed to look professional and capable, and she was the first to admit that blush, lipstick and mascara made her look a little older, a little less like a fresh-faced teenager than she normally did. Just as repainting her nails from purple enamel to clear polish made the professional image more complete. She told herself firmly that she wasn't worried about what Trent thought personally. She was simply trying to give herself whatever advantage she could now that she needed some extra income.

Hurrying out the front door, she grimaced at the summer sun, still forceful even at this hour of the evening. Maybe luck would be with her and she could at least arrive without having sweated off her careful grooming. It wasn't until she was halfway to Trent's house that she realized she'd left the directions—along with Trent's number—on the bed, and he had mentioned his phone was unlisted.

Gritting her teeth, she turned around and headed back, praying she wouldn't get stopped as she skirted the speed limit. In the end, she reached Trent's neighborhood only a little late. Maybe he wouldn't notice.

As she passed through the wrought-iron and stone archway that spanned the entry to the subdivision, she slowed down considerably. Any neighborhood this Yuppie was bound to have the requisite 2.4 children per household running around.

She snorted softly as a pair of identically clad joggers passed her on the sidewalk, their glances at her beat-up car expressing their concern as to what she might be doing on their side of town. Even the two fur balls running alongside stared at her. She wondered how their owners had trained them to do that.

The gate to Trent's place was open, and several cars lined the large driveway. She parked and headed for the front door, more than a little impressed. Somehow she guessed that no matter how old she got or how far she moved from the Buda, Texas, of her youth, she would always be awed by obvious wealth displayed in elegant, understated ways such as this.

Point in fact, she was much more impressed than she wanted to be. Her earlier musing proved correct—Trent *did* live in the house of her dreams.

The lines were elegant. Soft, draping curtains covered the many windows, back-lit by a warm and welcoming glow. She would have picked the same natural rock on the face of the house, and the steeply sloping roof promised at least one room with a vaulted ceiling.

The front porch was laden with green plants, and she couldn't stop herself from touching one to make sure it was real. She was surprised at the depth of her relief that, indeed, the greenery was alive.

The doorbell was answered by none other than seaman Joey. After announcing that his mother was in the kitchen, and pointing in the general direction of the back of the house, her erstwhile guide took off down the hallway toward the "beep-twiddle-beep" of a video game in progress.

With a shrug, Melodie headed through the house, breathing deeply the soft essence of flowers. Along with her other mistaken preconceptions regarding Trent, Melodie added decorating to her list. She'd been expecting dark leather, but found instead beige and soft blue fabrics. The carpet was deep and luxurious, though—she'd been right about that.

The house was filled with sound. In addition to the hidden video game, a stereo somewhere was playing soft rock favorites that mingled with laughter from down the hall to her left. She assumed the mixture of voices were the other members of the video team Trent had mentioned.

Melodie wound her way through the living room, assuming she was going in the right direction, and finally located the kitchen. She was delighted to find Bridgette exactly as she'd expected the parent of an urchin like Amber to be: petite, with her light brown hair pulled back in a swinging ponytail, and a bright, sweet smile. The mother was as warm and pleasant as the daughter, and it was easy to tell that Amber would be equally beautiful when she grew up.

"Amber talks about you all the time," Bridgette offered as she shook Melodie's hand and returned to slicing tomatoes. "She just loves dance class and is absolutely sure she's going to be a prima ballerina when she grows up."

Melodie chuckled. "Don't worry. As soon as she hits the tomboy stage, she'll want to be a fireman."

Bridgette smiled in return. "Oh, I'm sure. But I just wanted you to know that I appreciate the attention you give her." Bridgette stopped cutting and cocked her head. "Not that she gives you any choice!"

"Are you talking about my sweet girl?" A deep voice preceded a tall, blond-haired man into the kitchen. He moved behind Bridgette, wrapping his arms around her waist to nuzzle her neck.

Both intrigued by their play and feeling intrusive, Melodie's stomach tightened as she watched the couple. She wasn't used to such open displays of affection.

"Glen, stop it!" Bridgette shrugged him off, her cheeks flushing a becoming pink. "Glen, this is Melodie. She's Amber's dance teacher."

Glen offered Melodie a firm handshake. "So you're the one responsible for the need for ballet slippers and tights in every conceivable color."

"Oh, no," Melodie defended herself with a laugh. "I don't have a dress code for class. The kids were supposed to bring home notes telling you that."

"I think Amber conveniently lost hers."

"Listen, Melodie," Bridgette interjected, "would you mind taking these buns out to the barbecue so Trenton can get them browning? If I can get Glen to leave me alone long enough, I'll finish the condiments."

The knot in Melodie's stomach pulled taut. What could she say?

"Uh, sure."

"Just go straight through there," Bridgette directed with a pickle in hand, "and out the sliding doors to the patio."

Taking the bag of buns, Melodie left as instructed.

Trenton heard the glass door slide open, but he was too busy fighting the flaming grill with his squirt bottle to turn around. "Just a second, brat. I'm a little busy right now."

When he turned, he pulled himself up short. The beautiful woman standing there certainly wasn't Bridgette. She bore a striking resemblance to the quirky dance teacher he'd met earlier in the afternoon, however.

And a smile was twitching at the corner of her mouth.

"I have to admit I haven't been called a brat by a relative stranger in a long time. People usually have to know me for at least a week."

Trenton felt chagrined. "I apologize for that. I thought you were Bridgette."

"Nope, just me with the buns."

Trenton had to bite his tongue to keep from saying, "And nice buns they are." He didn't know Melodie yet, and sometimes people were taken off guard by his humor. Not to mention that, from their conversation this afternoon, Melodie obviously thought him something of a stuffed shirt. He wanted to relieve her of that impression, but not by changing the image to a sexist jerk.

She stepped forward, a little awkwardly, which struck him as odd. He found everything about her graceful, just as he'd expect in a dancer. Now that she was out of that baggy T-shirt and those wild leggings, he could see that his suspicions were indeed correct. Her sleeveless shirt revealed sleek, toned arms and an elegant neck. Her wrap skirt hugged slender hips, as well as the long legs he'd admired earlier, pigs and all.

Hearing the grill sizzle warningly behind him, he hurried forward to take the bread.

"Why don't you grab something to drink and have a seat?" He motioned with his tongs toward a cooler at the end of the benches built into the perimeter of the deck.

A length of her hair fell over her shoulder as she chose a cola from the ice. With the sunset behind her, and the breeze playing with her long tresses, she looked as though she could be posing for a commercial. He was sure he wouldn't be the only man to buy that brand of soda.

Suddenly his mouth felt dry. "Would you mind grabbing a root beer for me?" He nodded toward the grill. "It keeps flaming up and I don't want to scorch the burgers."

A moment later, as she handed him the chilled can, his fingers touched hers just for a second. It sent a jolt up his arm. Funny. He hadn't noticed how small the deck was before now. He'd entertained twenty or thirty people before and it had never felt this close.

And quiet. He'd turned off the outside speakers to enjoy the crickets and cicadas, but now the silence wrapped around him.

He cleared his throat. "Did you have any trouble finding the place?"

"None at all." She glanced around the deck. "Why are you out here by yourself?"

He flipped a patty and looked back at her. "Although the breeze makes it tolerable out here, everybody else likes the air conditioning. Besides, I just bought the newest version of Space Warriors from Planet Ten, and everyone's trying to beat my high score."

"You play video games?"

Her expression was nothing short of amazed. He barked a laugh. "Sure, why not?"

In the fading sunlight, he thought she blushed, but he wasn't certain. "I don't know. I . . . didn't take you for the video type."

His grin widened. "Just what type did you take me for?"

She smiled back. "Oh, somehow I imagined you spending an intimate evening with six or seven law books and a stack of legal pads."

Trenton exaggerated a wince. "Sounds like I need to work on my image."

She remained enigmatically silent.

He tried again. "I'm glad you could make it after all. What made you change your mind?"

"The idea intrigues me," she said, her face brightening. "I think I was taken off guard this afternoon. When I had a minute alone to let it all sink in, I realized I'd spoken too hastily at Kidstravaganza."

The grill chose to flame up again before he could reply. "Yow!" he yelped, snapping his hand away from the danger. He grimaced and nodded toward rust on the grill. "I'm glad the neighborhood association hasn't been by for an inspection, or I'd be in big trouble."

Again, surprise registered on her face. Had he really made that bad of a first impression? Did she think he had no sense of humor at all?

Every time he glanced at her, he experienced her viscerally. His lungs constricted, or his gut went taut, or his legs tightened. He found it all rather interesting since he'd been around some of the most beautiful women in the city, and none of them had had this effect on him.

He was suddenly having trouble remembering why he couldn't put her on his candidate list because he felt certain that somehow, some way, he was going to have to kiss those noncandidate lips. As much as he knew he needed his next breath, he would have to know the taste of her just one time before they went their separate ways. Although the end to his bachelorhood was imminent, it wasn't a fait accompli yet! He wouldn't mind spending some of his remaining free time with a beauty like Melodie. In fact, his fingers itched to run through that mass of molten flame cascading down her back. He guessed it would reach to her beautiful behind when let out of the elegant twist she'd spun it into, and he had every intention of confirming his suspicion as soon as the situation allowed.

His conscience twinged. When she'd been dressed in purple tie-dye and piggy leggings, he had immediately assumed she was flighty and inappropriate for the video. Even when they'd talked at the pizza parlor, he'd liked her more and more but still had been relieved when she'd declined an interest. Now, however, faced with this vision, he was forced to admit he had judged her on surface evidence. He, of all people, should know better than that.

When she glanced nervously at her fingernails—which he noticed were missing the purple enamel—he knew he must have been staring. It made her uncomfortable.

"I'm sorry. I didn't mean to be rude," he said.

She shrugged and flipped her hair over her shoulder. "Don't worry about it. I should expect your confusion after the way I was dressed this afternoon."

He matched her chuckle. "I must admit, I don't think I've ever seen anything quite like that get-up."

The corners of her eyes wrinkled as she smiled. It was charming.

"Now you'll have to forgive me for being rude, but you could use a casual consultant." Her eyes raked down his sports shirt and cutoffs.

"What?" he asked with pretended affront. "You don't like my outfit?"

"It'd be perfect if you'd put on a faded, holey jersey. But the collared shirt thing..." She shook her head despairingly.

Trenton guessed he wouldn't have to worry about whether she'd express her opinion or not if she joined the video team.

She took a sip of her drink.

Trenton finished piling the burgers on a platter and started toasting the buns.

The sound of the door gliding open caught their attention. Bridgette came out, holding hands with Glen.

"Everything's on the table. You about ready?"

In answer, Trenton handed Glen the huge platter of burgers. After taking the last set of buns off the grill, he shut off the gas and carried that platter himself.

Glancing back toward Melodie, he jerked his head toward the house. "Come on. Let's eat."

The ensuing moments were chaotic. Melodie was introduced to Ronald, Juan and Cassie, Bridgette's teammates. Ronald, she learned, was the cameraman, Juan the marketing director and Cassie did the still photography, specifically for the video jacket. Bridgette was the producer.

Amber was obviously feeling no ill effects from her upset stomach earlier for she was in the middle of the big melee of hands reaching for mayo and mustard and lettuce and pickles and chips.

A little intimidated, Melodie waited for the crowd to clear before fixing her plate and following the trail of people out of the kitchen. Bridgette was sitting on the floor, leaning back against Glen's legs. Ronald and Juan were in the easy chairs, and Cassie had claimed the other end of the couch by Bridgette. The kids were using the coffee table to support their plates, and Trenton was sitting on the step down into the sunken area.

Feeling awkward, she joined Trenton on the step, leaving a wide gap between them. Almost as if Amber had sensed her nervousness, the child hurried over and claimed Melodie's lap. Melodie didn't mind a bit, moving her plate to the floor beside her and her drink out of Amber's range. She helped the blond dynamo get settled and eat while she listened to the discussion in the center of the room.

Topics flew almost too fast for her to follow, among them being the times for their next several meetings, as well as a rapid back-and-forth discussion on the location for the filming of the first run-through.

Juan startled her when he looked at her and said without preamble, "So, what do you think of the idea?"

Choking on a chip, Melodie had to take a long drink before answering. When Trent started to move toward her, she waved him away while she patted Amber's arm to reassure the worried child. "I'm okay." She turned back to Juan. "I think it's great. You've got a market that's new, and your timing is excellent."

"Did Trenton fill you in on our concept?"

Melodie nodded.

Bridgette sat forward, excitement shining in her face. "I thought we could use different-aged kids. Say, maybe start with the younger ones for warm up, and as the exercises get more difficult, use older and older kids."

Melodie struggled to keep her expression neutral. She was afraid she was being a little pushy. Then she made the mistake of looking at Trent, and the encouragement she saw in his eyes made her mind go blank.

Great! Now she'd really look like a ding bat.

Four

"Go ahead, Melodie," Trenton urged her. "Tell us what you're thinking. That's what this meeting is for."

She swallowed to cover a second or two and her thoughts returned. "Well, it just struck me that you might be trying to do too much. Younger kids might be willing to relate to the older ones, but older kids consider anyone younger than themselves inferior. I'm not sure you could keep an older group focused."

Bridgette made a face at Trenton. "That's just about what he said. I told him he didn't know what he was talking about because he doesn't have kids."

"Score one for me," Trenton said lightly, licking his finger and making an imaginary mark in the air.

Bridgette ignored him. "Do you have any other ideas?"

"I'll admit my marketing experience is pretty narrow, but I'd try to target a specific age group and gear my class around it."

"So pick one age and stick with it," Glen chimed in.

"Or specifically segment an entire routine to several different ages," Melodie offered as a compromise.

Heads around the room nodded approvingly.

For some reason, Glen's earlier teasing about ballet slippers came to mind, and an idea struck her. "Has anyone thought about accessories?"

"Like mats or weights?" Ronald asked around a mouthful of burger.

"Sort of," Melodie said. "I'm sure your research has already told you this, but little girls are more susceptible to the extras, so I was thinking more along the line of sweatbands and wrist bands." She waved her hands, interrupting herself. "No, wait. I've got it. Ribbon wands!"

"That's a great idea!" Bridgette nearly spilled her drink as she rose up on her knees. "I can't believe I didn't think of it before, considering how much stuff like this I've bought in the last year. We could do a whole segment with little girls in different colors, each with her headband matching her ribbon."

Amber squealed in delight at the idea, squirming from Melodie's lap to jump in excitement. Melodie tried to block the rain of grape soda that came out of Amber's cup, but it was no use. Trent reacted more productively, lunging to take the cup from Amber's hand.

Amber turned toward Melodie, her smile fading when she realized what she'd done.

Melodie glanced down and saw three large blots of purple spreading toward each other across her silk tank top. Tears began spilling down Amber's cheeks.

"I'm sorry, Miss Melodie. I didn't mean to—"

"It's okay, sweetheart," Melodie reassured Amber, putting a gentle hand on her shoulder. "You were just excited. Please don't worry. It will wash."

Actually Melodie had serious doubts the purple would come out of the silk, but if it didn't, it wouldn't be the end of the world.

Melodie felt Trenton's gaze on the back of her neck. How she could tell his look from any of the rest of the folks in the room, she couldn't say, but feel it she did.

She glanced at him and confirmed that he was watching her. Intently.

Bridgette commanded her attention again. "Melodie, I'm so sorry about your blouse. Promise me you'll send me the cleaning bill?"

"Really, it's all right," she said, trying to gloss over the incident. "Let's just get back to the meeting. Please."

"Well, all right. I think the only thing left, then, is to see if you'll join the team. I just know you'll be perfect."

A chorus of voices agreed with Bridgette.

Melodie had to laugh. Now she knew exactly who Amber got her spontaneity from. "Conditionally, I'll say yes."

After a unanimous round of approving nods, everyone began to move. Melodie watched, bewildered, as the crowd took their plates to the kitchen as though everything was finished. She had a hundred questions to ask, but when she looked beside her, Trenton was gone.

"Miss Melodie, come see my room."

"It's not your room, you dope. It's just a guest room."

Amber placed indignant hands on her hips and rounded on her older brother. "Uncle Trenton says it's my room whenever I'm here, you... you dummy."

"Hey, now," Uncle Trenton said, appearing in the nick of time. "No name-calling or you won't be able to spend the night. You know the rules."

Amber lifted her nose and turned her back on her sibling to concentrate on Melodie. "I wanna show you my namaginerie."

Melodie glanced at Trenton. He was shaking his head indulgently. "She brings a menagerie over when she spends the night. Swears she can't sleep without them."

Amber was pulling her across the room as Trenton explained. "I'll be right back," Melodie assured him and let Amber lead her down the long hallway. She passed a room that had been turned into a TV/stereo/computer library. She envied Trenton his space.

Amber turned into the next room, releasing Melodie's hand to race across the floor and jump into the middle of a bed covered with stuffed animals.

Melodie made a place for herself on the edge and listened attentively.

"This is Muffy, and she's a doggy," Amber explained, holding up a poodle in a fifties-style circle skirt. Lilly, the black-faced lamb, was adorned in a calico dress and sunbonnet.

Every animal had a special name and outfit, and Melodie knew she'd be there half the night if she had to learn each one. While she was wondering how to extricate herself without hurting Amber's feelings, Trenton came to the rescue.

"All right, you little con artist. You know it's time for bed. Go brush your teeth and put your jammies on."

"But I'm not finished inneroducing Miss Melodie yet."

Trenton folded his arms over his chest in his best "I'm serious" pose. "She's met enough for tonight. You can introduce her to the rest of the gang next time."

Acting as though her world had just fallen apart, Amber took a pair of pajamas from a pink overnight bag sitting on the bay window seat. With her toothbrush in the other hand, she shuffled out the door and down the hall.

Melodie let out a giggle. "That child is priceless."

"Yeah, and we have to be careful because she's starting to take advantage of it."

"She'll be fine. She's just a happy, healthy four-year-old."

Something intense passed across Trenton's face. Something that spoke to her without words. Something that reached deep inside her and touched the little girl still living there who would have given anything to have a room full of toys and the obvious love of the adults around her.

Amber returned in record time, teeth bright and white, decked out in soft pink pajamas with lace adorning the collar. She jumped back onto the bed.

Melodie stood and moved out of the way as Trenton pulled back the comforter and motioned the child under. "You go to sleep. Your mom will be here in a minute."

"Uh-uh. She kissed me night-night in the hall and said she'd see you 'morrow."

"Oh. Well then, good night." He placed a kiss on her forehead.

"'Night." She waited almost the span of an entire second before sitting up. "I'm thirsty."

"Not a chance, little lady. Lie down."

She flung herself backward with a huff. In the next second she was up again. "Read me a story."

"Amber..."

Even Melodie could hear the warning note in his voice.

She lay back with less drama this time. "Can Miss Melodie kiss me night-night?"

Trenton looked at Melody as if to say, "It's up to you."

With Trenton in the way, she moved to the other side of the bed. "Will you go to sleep if I do?"

Amber promised with a nod.

Brushing Amber's bangs back with a gentle hand, Melodie placed a kiss on the child's forehead. When Amber's little arms reached around her neck for a hug, Melodie clenched her eyes against sudden, hot tears. She'd hugged this child and countless others before, but somehow, in this moment, the setting slipped past all her rigidly guarded barriers.

"Good night, princess," Melodie swallowed and said.

Maybe she was just tired, but all at once she was overwhelmed with sadness that she would never have a little princess of her own to tuck in. When she glanced across the bed at Trenton, her knees nearly gave way. Incredulously, as she looked into his eyes, their souls touched. As the sensation exploded through her body, she couldn't breathe, she couldn't move, yet her heart raced.

"Good night," Amber whispered back, breaking the moment and giving in to a yawn.

Trenton turned out the light behind them. As they walked back down the hall, she felt off balance, weak. Trenton, too, seemed distracted and unusually awkward. When he stopped by the computer room, he held on to the door as if he needed the support. "Just a few more minutes, buddy, then it's your turn for lights out."

"Okay," Joey acknowledged, never taking his eyes off the screen. Joey, being ever so much older, had a later curfew.

When they reentered the living room, Melodie felt her heart jump. They were alone.

"Where'd everyone go?" Melodie asked, her already-fragile reserve fading even more. "We were in Amber's room only for a few moments."

"Bridgette and Glen had a 9:20 movie they wanted to see, so they had to get going. The rest of the gang decided to take off, too, and regroup tomorrow."

"Oh." She didn't know what else to say.

"Did you want to ask me some questions?"

She did, but at the moment she was in sensory overload. All she wanted to do was go home and try to sort out everything that had happened.

"I do, but I've about reached my limit for tonight. Can I get together with you tomorrow?"

"Sure. We usually meet around seven to seven-thirty each night during the week, but since tomorrow's Saturday, we're meeting at two o'clock at Bridgette's. Is that all right?"

"That's great."

Retrieving her purse, she headed for the door, feeling awkward again as she waited for him to write down directions to Bridgette's house.

"Shall I walk you to your car?" Trenton offered as he held open the glass screen.

"No, please. That's not necessary." She fidgeted with the strap of her purse. "Well, thank you again for the invitation."

Hoping he wouldn't notice it shaking, she held out her hand, which he wrapped in the warmth of his long, strong fingers. "Thank you for coming. I think this is going to work out nicely."

"I hope so." She took her hand back and headed toward the driveway. "I'll see you tomorrow."

"Tomorrow."

He made it sound like a long-awaited rendezvous. Her stomach fluttered again.

As she got into her car, she noted he still stood in the doorway, watching. It wasn't until she had started her engine and was driving away that he closed the door.

Melodie followed Bridgette into the tiny kitchen that reflected more of the country-charm theme Bridgette had chosen for her small house. Saturday-afternoon sunshine streamed through white ruffled curtains covering the window over the sink, and every available nook and cranny displayed some kind of knick-knack.

"Your home is lovely, Bridgette," Melodie said as she started filling glasses with ice. She made the comment in all sincerity, even though the decor wasn't what she would have chosen for herself.

"Thanks!" Bridgette beamed. "Of course, if it weren't for Trenton, I'd be in some cramped apartment."

She cast a glance through the doorway to where her brother stood chatting with Ronald and Cassie.

"My big brother is such a softy. He knew there was no way I could afford a house on my salary so he insisted I rent this place from him for less than what I'd pay for an apartment. He says he wasn't able to keep it leased, which we both know is a big lie. Still, it makes him feel better that the kids and I are on this side of town."

"He does seem very protective," Melodie noted with humor.

Bridgette snorted. "That's an understatement. It's just going to kill him when—"

Melodie looked at her curiously but refrained from asking any questions that might embarrass them both. She liked the vivacious young woman. Still, Melodie didn't feel comfortable prying into Bridgette's life.

Letting her thoughts drift, Melodie mentally reviewed the results of today's meeting. Besides updating the schedule through the shooting of the dress rehearsal, Trent had covered a revised financial projection for the video. Melodie calculated that if she was careful with her meager savings, and found a roommate soon, she could squeak by until the first anticipated revenue materialized.

Bridgette came out of her reverie first, giving a little laugh as she handed Melodie the pitcher of tea from the refrigerator.

"Sorry," she said sheepishly. "I tend to zone out at the oddest times these days."

"Don't worry about it," Melodie reassured her, adding a friendly squeeze to Bridgette's shoulder.

Bridgette paused as she put a sugar bowl and spoons on the wicker tray waiting on the counter. Almost as if she couldn't help herself, she continued her confidences. "It's just that Glen is getting so serious. He's considering a job in Chicago and he wants to get married right away. But when I think about leaving Trenton, it tears me up."

Melodie shifted her feet uncomfortably. "I know this is unsolicited advice, but you can't live your life for your brother. You need to find your own happiness."

"That's true, and Trenton would be the first to agree. But he's done so much for me. He literally saved my life, you know."

No, Melodie didn't know, but it hardly surprised her. In fact, she wouldn't be surprised if she found out he had a unicorn grazing in his backyard. Or better yet, a destrier in full battle vestments. Surely somewhere in his house a suit of armor lay in wait.

"I was so stupid," Bridgette said absently. "You see, our parents were killed in a car wreck when I was three. Trenton was thirteen. An aunt raised us, but Trenton was in college when I hit my teens and turned into the brat from hell. He was the perfect kid—great grades, never in trouble, class president, et cetera. I, on the other hand, decided that I could do anything I darn well pleased with impunity." Bridgette grimaced wryly, meeting Melodie's eyes. "I was wrong."

Melodie nodded, understanding more than her new friend could ever know.

"Anyway, I ended up married to a total jerk at nineteen. The hitting didn't start until Amber was born, though."

"Oh, Bridgette. I'm so sorry."

"Believe it or not, the whole time Trenton tried to get me to open my eyes, but it wasn't until my ex started in on Joey that I woke up. Trenton came and got us, put me back in school and showered love on the kids." Bridgette sighed. "He's going to be a great daddy. I just hope this scheme of his works out."

Melodie gave her head a little shake. Bridgette had changed subjects so fast, she couldn't keep up.

"Pardon?"

"Sorry. I changed horses midstream, didn't I? I should finish by saying that if Trenton was settled, I wouldn't be so worried about moving. But he has this crazy notion that he needs to find a 'suitable' wife and start a family. I'm afraid if I'm not around, he'll marry someone who's perfect according to his computer calculations, but who'll make him miserable."

Melodie was stunned into another moment of silence. Serena may have mentioned Trent was on the marriage market, but it never occurred to her that the guy was this serious.

She turned to Bridgette. "Wait a minute. Do you mean he has just decided it's time to get married and, *poof,* he's going to do it?"

Bridgette nodded sadly. "I've told him you can't shop for a bride like a head of lettuce, but he doesn't believe me that he should wait until he's head over heels in love. He says that only happens in the movies."

At Melodie's skeptical expression, Bridgette barked a laugh. "You don't know my big brother, Melodie.

Once his mind is set on something, he goes for it, and no power on earth can stop him. He's been that way since he was a kid.''

"Amazing."

"Yes, he really is. He's a wonderful man and would be the best husband in the world.''

Melodie's lip quirked. "I have the feeling you might be a bit biased on this subject.''

"No, really," Bridgette assured her earnestly. "Trenton is a great guy, if a little overfocused.'' She stopped again, and looked at Melodie as if seeing her for the first time.

Melodie's gut meter immediately pegged into the danger zone. "Bridgette, I don't know *you* that well, either, but the look you're giving me is making me nervous.''

Bridgette's smile was almost beatific. "It's ideal!''

"What is?''

"Unlike my brother, I've learned to trust my instincts, and right now they're telling me that you're perfect for him.''

"Bridgette, listen—''

"I know it's sudden, but I already feel close to you. I'd feel disloyal telling you all this otherwise. You see, Trenton has no spontaneity in his life, and if left to his own devices, he's going to pick some woman who's more worried about their status at the country club than whether Trent's happy.''

Melodie frowned in confusion. "Again, I point out that I don't know him well, but he doesn't strike me as the kind of guy who'd go for the elitist type.''

Bridgette gave a horrified gasp. "Oh, not at all! It's just that he's assembled this list of qualities, as though he's going to stir this woman up from a recipe. He truly doesn't believe in the grand passion and thinks he should go after a wife like he interviews associates for his law firm. All the women he meets are fast-track, A-types who are just like him.''

"Well, if that's what he needs...."

"No, no, no! Whether he knows it or not, he does *not* need a female version of himself—all schedules and planner notebooks. He needs someone like you.''

"Me! What in the world makes you think I—''

"You're perfect! You're down to earth, you're beautiful—''

"Bridgette, please—''

"You're funny and intelligent. And—''

"Bridgette—''

A shadow passed over Melodie's shoulder. She didn't have to turn around. She knew who it was.

"Funny and intelligent?'' Trenton asked, his deep voice running down her spine like a drop of warm water. "Are you talking about me again?''

Bridgette gave him a disgusted look. "No, I am not talking about you, you egomaniac. I was talking about Melodie.''

"Oh.'' He managed to convey amused disappointment in the single syllable. "Well, I'm hurt, but I agree.''

Melodie felt her face burn.

"Please,'' she managed in a strangled voice, "stop.''

Melodie should have been ready when Bridgette changed directions again without a pause, ordering Trenton to take the glasses to the living room. Bridgette followed in his wake as if she'd planned it this way all along. She stopped at the doorway and looked back.

"Well, are you coming or not?''

* * *

By ones and pairs, the group left Bridgette's house. The meeting had gone rather well, Trenton thought as he walked Melodie to her car. Except for the odd looks Melodie had given him when she'd followed Bridgette out of the kitchen, and the equally odd smiles Bridgette threw his way during the course of the afternoon, everything had gone much as he'd expected.

Amber, he noticed, hadn't let go of Melodie's hand for the last twenty minutes. He decided it was a diversionary tactic. Amber knew that if she begged sweetly in the presence of a witness, he was more likely to cave in and let them come over to swim. Of course, as soon as Joey had heard him waver, he'd closed in for the kill. With both kids pleading, and Melodie's eyes lit with humor, how could he say no?

Bridgette and Glen had just pulled away to take advantage of some rare alone time when Trent's cellular phone chirped. Unzipping his day planner, he grabbed the small unit and apologized to Melodie with a smile as he answered.

As soon as he heard the voice on the other end, his heart sank.

"Penelope, I'm so sorry. I forgot about the charity auction tonight. I have my niece and nephew. I'm afraid I—"

He broke off as Melodie touched his arm. "I'll take them," she whispered.

"Penelope? Hang on for just a second."

He put his thumb over the tiny mouthpiece and said, "That's nice, but I really couldn't ask."

"I don't mind at all."

Trenton eyed her car dubiously and felt sheepish when she laughed.

"I'll even go over to your house and stay with them. I'd rather not take them in my rust bucket anyway."

Embarrassed to be caught out, Trenton gave in graciously. "Thank you." Putting the phone back to his ear, he said, "Penelope? Yeah, I've got it covered.... That's a great idea...are you sure you wouldn't mind...? That's great.... I'll meet you at my house in about an hour and a half. Bye."

He could tell Melodie was struggling against a smile as he put up the cellular.

"Shame on you, Trent. Forgetting a hot date."

He took her teasing with good-humored grace. "It's not a hot date. It's a charity auction benefiting Aids Services of Austin. My firm does some *pro bono* work for them. I just forgot all about it."

"Well, go and have a good time. The kids and I'll be fine."

"Are you sure about this? I'll order you guys some take-out. Your choice."

After Melodie's final reassurance, he led the way home. An hour later, he was clean and shaved, cursing his bow tie and hunting for the cummerbund he'd sworn he'd laid on the bed.

He stopped his frantic searching and stood with his hands on his hips. "Amber!" he shouted down the hall. After a moment, a doll appeared at about ankle level from around the corner. Not only did her white dress bear a surprisingly familiar train of black-pleated satin, but an equally familiar diamond tie tack held it in place.

"Isn't she pretty, Uncle Trenton?" Amber asked, finishing Barbie's walk of honor up her uncle's leg.

"Gorgeous," he affirmed, tongue in cheek, as he divested Barbie of her accoutrements, putting his tie tack on his dresser and his cummerbund around his waist.

"You look pretty, too, Uncle Trenton."

He bent over to plant a kiss on the top of her head. "Thanks, munchkin. Have you had dinner?"

"The pizza's not here yet. Miss Melodie said I had to be a patient. Do I really have to go to the doctor?"

He chuckled. "No, sweetie, she means you just have to wait a little longer."

"Oh. I was wonderenen why, 'cause I'm not sick."

Joey appeared in the doorway. "You may not be sick, but you sure are a pain," he said, coming into the room. "Hey, Uncle Trenton, you look like a penguin." He held his arms against his sides and flapped his hands like little wings.

Trenton gently cuffed his nephew on the shoulder. "Very funny."

The doorbell rang and Joey and Amber locked excited eyes.

"Pizza!" they shouted, barreling down the hall to answer the summons.

Trenton finished dressing in peace, joining the trio around the coffee table as he waited for Penelope.

"Want some, Uncle Trenton?" Joey offered magnanimously, his mouth full.

"Don't talk with food in your mouth. And no, thank you." He caught Melodie's attention. "I do appreciate this, you know."

Her smile was genuine, and he caught a gleam of something in her eyes as she looked at him, a hint of something that made his pulse do a little skip.

"You're welcome. And that's the last time you can thank me." She wiped her hands on a napkin and assessed him with her head tilted slightly. "You look great. They'd probably make a lot more money if they auctioned you."

Trenton felt flustered, something that was rare for him. Although he hardly knew her, her quirky comments were already familiar. She'd tossed off enough one-liners to keep them all in stitches. But somehow this comment made him wish he was spending the evening on the floor with her and the kids, eating pizza and drinking soda instead of going for champagne and caviar at a ritzy hotel.

The doorbell rang again, and it wasn't a stretch for Trenton to guess that it was for him this time. He reluctantly broke his eye contact with Melodie and headed for the door.

He invited Penelope in and made the introductions.

Amber gasped and jumped up, racing toward Penelope. "You look just like my Dream Girl Barbie," she said in awe, reaching for an enticing piece of black lace.

Penelope took a quick step back and grabbed Amber's hand. "Don't touch. Okay, honey?"

Trenton thought her too-high falsetto sounded absurd. Penelope was a stunningly beautiful, intelligent woman. Why, then, did she think she had to talk to Amber like a two-year-old? She seemed petrified Amber was going to touch her with greasy fingers and Trenton fought down a surge of irritation. Her fear might be justified, but she didn't have to treat Amber as though she had the plague.

Stroking a hand down Amber's silky hair, he distracted her. "Go finish your dinner, sweetie. I'll see you in the morning."

"Is Miss Melodie sleeping over?"

Penelope arched a perfectly curved brow.

Trenton tried to make light of the innocent comment. "No, she'll go home when I get back."

"Can she stay over next time?"

A glance between the quirky redhead with an amused smile and the cool blonde with a bemused frown offered him no help.

"Amber," he said sternly, squatting down, "go finish your pizza. Now."

Confused, Amber did as she was told, shrugging her shoulders at Melodie as she passed by. Trenton contained the smile tugging at his mouth. "Good night, all," he offered, turning and putting a solicitous hand under Penelope's elbow.

"You kids have a good time," Melodie called out behind him.

He felt Penelope stiffen and fought an urge to chuckle. He sobered when he realized it would be quite a blow to Penelope if he revealed any hint of his wish that the evening were already over.

He stumbled mentally. This had never happened before. He liked going out. He even liked Penelope. To be truthful, he was considering Penelope quite seriously.

So why did his thoughts stay home with the redhead?

Five

A week after her impromptu baby-sitting job, Melodie sat at her desk, still exasperated with herself. All she'd done was open her mouth before thinking—something not uncommon to her—and then she'd found herself keeping Amber and Joey for Trent's big evening out with the blond bombshell.

Seeing him in a tux had almost been worth feeling like a school kid, awestruck when he'd ushered the most beautiful woman she had ever seen into the room. For a moment, Melodie had wanted to sink into the floor and hide her blue jeans and T-shirt. Then she'd reminded herself that it didn't matter that the outfit Penny-kins had been wearing probably cost more than an entire month of her own salary. And it didn't matter that every blond hair and every stroke of the woman's makeup was flawless. And Melodie refused to admit that she secretly hoped those diamond earrings were so heavy they stretched those perfect lobes.

Melodie had decided on the spot that she hated Penelope. In fact, the feeling still held. She pretended that she didn't feel a pang, deep in her heart, when she acknowledged Penny was the perfect date for Trent. The kind of date she could never be in a million years. One had to be born into privilege to have that kind of suave, sophisticated demeanor.

Shaking away her errant thoughts, Melodie forced herself into the present, glancing around her tiny office to focus herself. She'd managed, until tonight, to keep too busy to think about how incredible Trent had looked in that tux. Only actors should look that good—and only then because they had make-up artists and wardrobe specialists to fool the eye. It was positively sinful for Trent to be that stunning without a girdle or shoulder pads or lifts in his shoes.

With an exasperated sigh, she looked at her notes again and made herself concentrate. She had reviewed her roster, recruited twelve students and worked out several routines. They had decided to go with the two groups—four-to-six- and seven-to-ten-year-olds—so her choreography had to keep their different physical abilities in mind, yet make the dances appear seamless.

Melodie was more anxious than she'd expected to be as she waited for the team to see her work-to-date. Luckily the job had kept her too preoccupied to worry much about Bridgette's bizarre announcement about her pairing up with Trent. Melodie could only hope that Bridgette had listened to her plea to forget whatever scheme was forming in her little matchmaking brain. Somehow Melodie doubted Bridgette had paid much attention to her.

Melodie wiped her palms down the leg of her sweatpants. She started to go change before the team arrived, but decided she was being foolish and admonished herself to calm down.

She glanced at the door for the hundredth time. Where was Theresa? She should have been there ten minutes ago with the outfits.

Costumes were one of the items on tonight's agenda. Theresa was a professional seamstress, a boon since her daughter was on the beauty-pageant circuit, and Melodie had enlisted Theresa to do a couple of mock-ups. The parents of the participants had agreed to pay for the outfits in return for extra copies of the video.

Melodie practiced a relaxation technique. It was bad enough that every time she looked at Trent she lost her breath. She didn't need to borrow more trouble by hyperventilating. In some ways, she resented his effect on her. The tuxedo incident was merely one example. Another was the incident at Saturday's meeting when everyone had gathered around her as she'd sketched costume ideas. Already edgy from Bridgette's comments, Melodie had felt stretched taut as a wire. Then Trent had moved to stand close against her left side, his breath warm on her neck. Her hands had shaken so badly, she'd had to tear up her first attempt and concentrate with all her might on her drawing.

She jumped when the door opened and released a sigh when she saw Theresa.

Her relief was short-lived, for the door opened again and the team filed in.

* * *

Trent came into the studio last, having graciously held the door. Amber hurried over to her friends while Joey took a seat in the observation area, his hand-held video game already beeping.

It must have been a late day at the office, for Trenton was wearing yet another perfectly cut suit with a crisp dress shirt and silk tie. This time the jacket was as black as his hair and it made him look elegant and professional. She decided it would be stating the obvious to say he looked sexy as all get-out. In fact, the more she saw him, the more she knew he was unaware of the presence he made in a room. It was innate, unpracticed.

She was surprised at the strength of her reaction, for she didn't usually go for the white-collar type. But Trent was more than just the stereotype. He might be driven, like Bridgette said, but he had a heart-stopping smile that made a woman believe he'd forget work when he was with her.

She had to find some way to bring her pulse under control. They were business partners. Period. Not that he'd be interested in someone like her—especially in light of Bridgette's revelation that he was bride hunting under some very strict guidelines. Guidelines that were clear with one glance at Perfect Penelope. But the fact remained that her unfettered imagination was getting in the way. The last thing on God's green earth she was interested in was a man looking for marriage. But if that were so, she couldn't explain why she thought about him such an inordinate amount of time.

Being thrown together almost every day certainly wasn't helping. Although the meetings were focused, they also served to intensify an intimacy that would have taken much longer to form under normal circumstances. The team already felt like family to her, although, to be honest, her thoughts toward Trenton were anything but sisterly.

Melodie took two plastic-covered hangers from Theresa and moved toward the team, smiling at everyone. "Hi, guys. The costumes just arrived. Let's go to my office and see what we've got."

Trenton took a position against the wall. Even though his financial backing was making the project possible, his ego was not so bloated that he felt the need to add his two cents' worth on every decision.

He agreed with the group that both beribboned creations were eye-catching—he'd known when he'd watched Melodie sketch them that they'd be great. He also agreed when the majority voted to go with the blue Lycra with big slashes of white and fuchsia.

It didn't take him long to notice that Melodie avoided his eye as much as possible. Other than a polite greeting, she concentrated her attention anywhere but on him, and he nearly smiled. She might be trying to avoid him, but there was no doubt that she was aware of him.

Good. He wanted it that way.

With the costume decision made, they took seats in the observation area to watch Melodie run the girls through their paces. Trenton had a hard time concentrating on the children as his eye kept slipping back to watch her move around in her torso-hugging leotard. Unfortunately, she was covered from the waist down in baggy sweatpants, but the contrast let his imagination run wild.

When he got his mind off her body and paid attention, it was clear from the short routines that Melodie had a true gift for working with children. Even to his untrained eye, she had real talent. She had natural grace and fluidity, and was certainly to be commended for her ability to keep six little girls focused on their dancing.

Ronald, ever the cameraman, pointed out that the girls turned their backs to the camera too often. Trenton instinctively wanted to defend Melodie, only to be grateful that he'd kept his mouth shut as he watched her think about the critique and agree. Melodie promised to redo the necessary segments and keep the advice in mind as she choreographed the future sections. He thought artists were supposed to be temperamental, veritable prima donnas with a work in progress, but once again Melodie was proving to be made from a different mold.

Crossing his arms over his chest, Trenton tapped a finger against his lips as he continued to watch.

Before it seemed possible, two hours had flown by. Parents had placed their orders with Theresa, and the team had left. Amber turned cranky, so she and Bridgette bowed out next. Joey, still absorbed in conquering an evil sorcerer, followed behind.

Melodie had been so busy straightening the studio, she didn't notice it was empty until she said good-bye to the last parent. Then the quiet struck her. She was used to the gradual decrease in activity and noise. What she wasn't used to was finding herself alone with a tall, dark, handsome man standing patiently for her by the door.

She forced a smile. "You don't have to wait for me."

"But I want to."

The sound of his voice reached her from across the quiet studio more completely than all the noise of the last hour. She'd been fairly successful in avoiding being alone with him the whole week, but now, obviously, he wasn't willing to be ignored any longer.

"Why?"

He smiled. It was a slow, sexy move that made her stomach somersault.

"Because you intrigue me."

Her fingers shook as she flipped the switch that plunged the back half of the room into darkness—and instantly regretted it. The reduced lighting gave the moment an even more intimate quality, so she hurried into her office.

"It isn't my intention to intrigue you," she informed him as crisply as she was able, considering how difficult it was to keep her knees and voice from trembling. She fumbled with her hip pack, keeping her eyes and hands busy, yet she knew without looking that he had moved the three steps from the front door to her office door and stood waiting. Even with the safety of her desk between them, she felt his overpowering presence.

Zipping her case, she strapped it around her waist with a snap.

"Look, Trent, I know I should be flattered, but the fact is that you and I are business partners now. Business and sex don't mix."

"Who said anything about sex?"

She started. "You said . . . I thought . . . I mean . . ."

"Don't get me wrong, I approve of the idea, although it is possible for a man and a woman to be just friends. I, however, like to get to know a woman before I take her to bed."

His arrogance was just the right touch to jar her out of her fluster. "Before you take *her* to bed? Good Lord, with an ego like that, where did I ever get the impression you were stuffy?"

Trenton leaned a shoulder against the jamb. "I'd like to know the answer to that, myself."

Melodie blushed instead of answering. She hadn't intended to actually say what she had. Now she felt as trapped by her words as by Trent blocking her doorway.

He wasn't going to let her off the hook.

"Why don't we talk about it over dinner?" he offered casually.

"I don't think that would be a good idea. Besides, it's late."

"It's only nine o'clock."

Melodie sighed and met his gaze squarely. "Why are you doing this?"

"I told you—"

"Oh, come on, Trent. I'm hardly your type and we both know it."

That enigmatic tilt to his lips was back. "And just what is my type?"

"You know, wealthy debutante, in the social register...."

"Don't you think I'm a little old for the debutante routine?"

"You're not even forty yet. You're prime meat."

"Well, thank you."

She gave him an exasperated look. "You know what I mean."

"Do I? It seems from the moment we met, you and I have misjudged each other."

This time she was intrigued. "Really? And how have you misjudged me?"

"Go to dinner with me and I'll tell you."

"That's bribery."

He nodded. "So it is. But you'll find that as a general rule, I always get what I set out for."

"And you'll use any means to do it?"

"Anything short of a felony."

"That leaves misdemeanors wide open, I guess."

His shrug was eloquent in its silence.

The gauntlet had been thrown. He obviously wasn't going to move until she answered him, and there was no way she was going to try to squeeze past him. She had no doubt that if she moved forward, challenging him to give way, he'd simply raise one of those dark brows and dare her to make him.

She tried one last tactic. "I'm in sweatpants and athletic shoes. I'm hardly dressed for dinner, especially with you looking like that."

She nodded toward him, indicating clearly that although he'd taken off his jacket and loosened his tie, he had hardly lowered himself to her level of casual.

Undaunted, Trenton waved away her argument. "We'll go to the Southwest Café, then."

"I've never been there."

"That makes it even better. We won't look out of place, I promise."

Her glance was dubious.

"Trust me."

Such simple words. Trust him. Surely she was presumptuous to assume his remark referred to anything more than his judgment on restaurants. Wasn't she?

"Oh, all right. I suppose I do need to eat."

He smiled at her as though she had just granted him his heart's desire. It served to knock away what little equilibrium she'd managed to reclaim.

He stepped sideways, indicating with a gallant wave for her to precede him out of the office. Left with no choice, she tried to put some confidence into her walk as she made her way to the door.

She should have been ready, but when his arm suddenly blocked her exit through the doorway, her heart stopped. Then when she looked up at him, so close to her, it started beating again. Too fast.

In another one of those moments usually reserved for the movies, she just stood there, immobilized, staring into his eyes. She waited, expectantly, as he lowered his mouth to hers and claimed her lips in a possessive kiss.

She might have been wrong about him being stodgy, but she had been sure he would be as methodical about kissing as he was about the rest of his life, especially with what Bridgette had revealed.

But oh, no. Here was where the soul of one Trenton James Laroquette lived. His lips on hers were an invitation to joy, his tongue a gentle, coaxing summons to experience the decadently sensual.

And the summons was so tempting, so irresistible, it scared her to death.

She wanted to pull away, but she couldn't. Trenton had tilted her chin up with his knuckles and was using that gentle touch to keep her still. He used her gasp of pleasure against her, delving with his tongue in a tender invasion of her mouth.

The spicy smell of his after-shave tickled her nose, and it was all she could do not to wrap her arms around his neck and pull him closer. She was terrified of what she would do if she actually traced that broad chest, felt the heat of his skin under her fingers.

After a million years, when he finally dropped his hand from her chin and pulled away, she took a shuddering breath. "Why did you do that?" she croaked.

"To get it out of the way. We've both been thinking about it and I thought, this way you'll anticipate me kissing you good-night instead of obsessing about it."

She choked on a laugh. "You're really incredible, you know that?"

"Thank you."

"That wasn't a compliment."

"It bothers you, doesn't it?"

"What? That you're arrogant and overbearing?" She shifted, the doorframe still hard against her back.

"That I'm confident. That I know what I want and I pursue it."

Melodie decided she needed to stop this nonsense here and now. Bridgette had already spilled the beans that he was wife hunting, and since she had no intention of ever being trapped in a marriage, on top of the fact that she was a walking example of what *wasn't* on his shopping agenda, there was no need for them to continue this topic.

"Actually," she informed him in deadly earnest, "I could care less what you pursue or don't pursue—as long as you leave me off your list."

Trenton was pleased that Melodie wasn't the kind to fill a drive with idle chatter. It wasn't that he couldn't drive and talk at the same time, but at this particular moment he was still reeling from his reaction to that kiss. The time spent alone, following her home to drop off her car, had not been enough for him to decompress.

And just what had she meant about leaving her off his list? Unlike some men, he'd never kept a list, or a little black book. He considered it juvenile. Why would she think such a thing?

He reminded himself, without false modesty, that he had kissed a fair number of women over the years. He'd enjoyed it. They'd enjoyed it. He'd made sure. He'd had entire evenings of enjoyable kissing and the activities that followed to a logical conclusion, which had all been eminently pleasurable, as well. But not once, not ever, had he been rocked to the bottom of his soul by a simple joining of his lips to a woman's.

Until tonight, when his contact with her succulent mouth had been broken, and he'd doubted his ability to form a complete sentence. He'd been amazed by the success of his less-than-brilliant retort. Her question—"Why did you do that?"—had been a silly one anyway. Because she was beautiful, of course. And because he could hardly breathe whenever he was near her. Because he couldn't get that apricot-peachy scent of her shampoo out of his mind.

He was sure she'd seen he was a fake, noticed that his pulse was racing, that his hands were shaking. Then again, maybe all those years of practicing law were paying off. Somehow he'd managed to convince her that he was confident—arrogant by her definition—and anything but a man who was reacting like a teenager in the midst of a hormone attack.

The truth was, he did have confidence. Both in his professional life and his personal one. He had always been intrigued by the elements of the chase. The hunt was entertaining, but had been predictable of late. At least he hadn't become jaded over the years, as some of his friends had.

But events of this evening had left him shaken. The kiss was supposed to have been an easy foray into flirtation.

Not a volcanic eruption.

Melodie played with the tails of the white dress shirt she wore loosely knotted around her waist. It was her favorite cover-up over her leotard. She supposed, since they'd gone to all the trouble to drop her car off at her house, that she should have run inside to change. But he'd said to trust him.

With a sigh of resignation, she snuggled back into the seat and turned her face into the gentle current coming from the air-conditioning vent. She traced a pattern on the plush cushion of her seat, enjoying the decadent feel and the comfortable quiet. At the same time, she hated being so impressed by his car. All her adult life she had rejected overt materialism, but even the click of the seat belt had sounded refined—not too loud, just confidently crisp. She closed her eyes and nearly moaned. She really was losing it.

Despite the late hour, the restaurant parking lot was full. So full, in fact, they had to take stools at the bar until a table could be bussed. Melodie wondered if this would be another Yuppie hangout where the food was expensive and the patrons posturing.

She found instead, as she glanced around the room, that everyone seemed to be having a good time. There were only a few brittle smiles and arrested gestures, and only one table where the parties looked like combatants. And Trent had been right. She saw every type of clothing, from designer label to basic grunge.

All in all she was pleasantly surprised.

"Can I get you something to drink?"

The bartender's voice made her jump, and then feel foolish. She tried to think fast. It wasn't just that this was Thursday and she usually saved her rare indulgences for the weekend. It was more that she was opposed to facing a room full of screaming children tomorrow with a splitting head. Adding, of course, that while this might not be a date, per se, she had no desire to fall face-first into her mashed potatoes either.

"Just some seltzer with a twist, please."

"And you, sir?"

"A beer."

As the bartender named the available choices, Melodie listed another surprise in her mental notebook.

Trenton looked at her, his smile sardonic. "Okay, what are you thinking?"

Melodie flushed but said truthfully, "Oh, I just wasn't expecting you to order beer. A glass of port wine, maybe, or something equally...um..."

"Stuffy?"

"I wasn't going to say that."

"No, but you were thinking it." He glanced at the waitresses. "I sure wish we'd get a table so I can pry the whole story out of you."

"Oh, so this *is* an interrogation disguised as a date?"

Melodie wished she could snatch the words back. When was she going to start thinking before she started talking?

As she expected, Trent hiked one of his thick, dark brows. "Ve haf vays of mekking you talk, young vooman."

Melodie chuckled. "I bet you do," she said under her breath. And she'd never admit it to him, but it might be a lot of fun to find out just what methods he had up his sleeve.

"So *is* this a date?" Trent mimicked in normal English.

"No, of course not," she said a trifle breathlessly. "I was just—"

"It would be fine with me if it was. In fact—"

"It was just a lame attempt at humor on my part. I'm sorry I even tried," she said, trying to divert him.

"Sounds to me more like you're worried about semantics. Why? Are you afraid I'll ask your sign or some other top secret info?"

Humor was always her best cover when she'd put her foot in her mouth or had started something she didn't want to finish.

With a laugh, she said, "If you ask my sign, I warn you I'll be forced to do something drastic."

"Sounds interesting. Tell me more."

"You're misbehaving, Trent."

"Oh, I haven't even started yet, believe me."

"That's what I'm afraid of. Since you aren't going to keep your end of the bargain, I'd say you've forfeited your dinner." She noticed a waitress heading for them, so she slid off her stool as if to head for the door.

Six

Trenton grabbed her arm in a gentle squeeze and tugged her back around to face him. "Oh, no, you're not getting away that easily." The chuckle he was so valiantly trying to contain burst out. "I give you my word of honor that I'll behave. And I won't ask your sign."

The waitress looked too busy to care about their strange exchange. She hurried them to a corner booth and promised to return shortly for their order.

It only took Melodie a moment to read the menu and make her selection. Folding her hands on the table, she reached inwardly for another smile and a dose of humor.

"I'm a Virgo."

"Congratulations."

"I just thought you should know."

"If you ever want any help changing that, I'd be happy to volunteer."

She paused. "I said Virgo, not virgin."

Trenton pretended to be insulted. "Don't get mad at me! You were the one who said we weren't discussing signs."

"We're not discussing it. I was just making a comment."

"If you say so."

"Now we're supposed to talk about family, right?"

"I don't know. Do you have a Robert's Rules of Conversation hidden somewhere that I don't know about?"

Melodie traced the condensation on her water glass with a fingernail. Finally she met his eyes. "Look, you might not have noticed, but I'm feeling a little awkward."

She expected him to tease her again. She tensed, waiting for his riposte. Instead, he reached across the table and took her hand, making her jump.

"Then what can I do to make this easier?"

Her pulse throbbed under his thumb as he gently stroked the inside of her wrist. She could hardly find her voice.

"I'm not sure there's anything you can do," she managed to say, taking her hand out of his reach. "Just being here makes me nervous, so I guess we'll have to make the best of it."

"I have to confess, Melodie. I'm confused."

Melodie tossed her head back. "Once again I confuse you. I don't know if I should be amused or insulted."

He ignored her and continued. "I mean, as beautiful as you are, surely dating is not a problem."

His compliment warmed her more thoroughly than hot cocoa on a winter's evening. She steeled herself against the delicious sensation. "I thought we established that this wasn't a date."

"I wasn't talking about tonight. I meant in general. You're single, you're vivacious, you're easy on the eyes... surely you get asked out all the time."

Melodie leaned forward conspiratorially, crooking her finger at him. "Let me let you in on a secret. I teach kids at day-care centers all day long. All evening, I teach dance at my studio with parents watching every move I make. The men I meet are usually the daddies of these little darlings, and somehow I think the mommies would get the tiniest bit perturbed if the daddies asked me out."

She sat back, took a sip of water and grimaced. "To be honest, I think a snail has a more active dating life than I do. Just about all my friends have paired off, as well, and it makes things... difficult sometimes."

"Why don't you get them to set you up?"

"Why would I want to?" she asked, perplexed. "Dating takes a lot of work."

"But the rewards can be great."

"If it's what you're looking for." She set her glass down with a thunk. "You know, this really isn't any of your business. I mean, I don't mind us getting to know each other a little better since we're business partners and all, but that doesn't entitle you entry into my private life. And just how did this conversation turn so personal so fast, anyway?"

"I don't know. It appears you and I are intent on skipping all the preliminaries and jumping straight into the thick of things."

She pinned him with a look. "Or maybe you just want it that way."

The look he returned made the air sizzle between them. "It wouldn't hurt my feelings in the slightest."

Her mouth went dry. She struggled to swallow.

He rescued her from a response by settling back in his seat and asking, "So, do you have any brothers and sisters?"

She sighed resignedly. "Do you really want to know?"

When his eyes traced her face, she felt that warmth again, spreading through her as though sunbeams danced along her veins.

"Yes," he answered softly. "I really do. I want to know everything there is to know about you."

She felt a blush start at her neck and move slowly upward.

She cleared her throat. "Well, I'm the youngest of two. My brother was a Marine. He was killed in the Gulf War."

"I'm sorry."

"Me, too. We weren't very close, but I loved him."

"What kept you distant? Age?"

"No, we were only three years apart. The long and short of it is, my parents adored Nathan and I think I was an oops. Their world revolved around him and I was pretty much just an extra item to pack into the station wagon."

Sympathy flashed across Trenton's face. It hit her harder than she could have imagined. His concern was so honest, tears welled in her eyes. She fought them away, unused to anyone reacting to the hurt she thought she kept well hidden whenever she had to tell this story. She did a quick mental review and was sure she'd delivered the story in the casual, it-doesn't-bother-me-anymore tone she'd worked hard to perfect.

"That must have hurt."

"Yeah, it did."

Fortunately he didn't pursue the subject, and the waitress returning for their orders offered an additional respite.

"What made you pursue dancing as a career?" Trenton asked as their conversation resumed.

"I'm not sure when the grand decision was made. I spent a lot of time with earphones on during Nathan's sport of the month. In high school I was in drill team and I majored in athletics in college. I sort of fell into teaching through a friend."

A frown marred Trenton's forehead. "Forgive me for playing armchair psychologist, but if your brother was such a jock, and you resented him, why in the world did you major in athletics? It seems like that would be the last thing you'd choose."

"That would be true, if life were logical. I spent my adolescence trying to get my parents' attention. Being an honors student didn't do it. Turning wild one year and nearly flunking out didn't do it. Somehow I decided that if I was as good an athlete as Nathan, that would do it. I carried a double major—botany and athletics."

She stopped as their salads were delivered and drinks refilled. "I had a friend ask me one time if that meant I was able to grow plants really fast."

"And you said?"

"Only the mold on the stuff in my refrigerator."

Trenton chuckled dutifully as he speared a bit of lettuce and sprouts. "I take it then that your attempt failed?"

"You could say that. Finally I got it through my thick skull that nothing I did was going to matter, so I formed a surrogate family with my friends."

Trenton was silent for a long time. Melodie fidgeted until she couldn't stand it anymore. "Hey, I don't mean to be such a depressing dinner partner. We can change the subject."

Her words seemed to jerk him out of his thoughts. "I'm sorry. It's not you. I was just thinking that I wasn't sure which was worse—having parents who didn't care about you, or no parents at all."

Melodie flushed. "I can see how you'd think my parents didn't care, but that isn't exactly true. We didn't have much money, but I was clothed and fed and had a few small luxuries. I just had none of their attention. They must have thought quality time meant sitting with them in the stadium." She forced down a bite of salad. "It doesn't matter."

He gave her a look that said "I doubt it," but he refrained from verbalizing his thoughts. She was grateful.

She toyed with her food again and decided it was time to turn the tables. "Now, about you. Bridgette mentioned you were orphaned when you were young."

"I was thirteen. The brat was three. My parents were both geology professors, and we were on our way to study sedimentary strata in the Grand Tetons."

Melodie made a sympathetic mew. "Hardly a thirteen-year-old's idea of a wild vacation."

"Actually," he said with a half shrug, "we were part of a group from the college. There were several kids my age, and some of the students were fun. We'd go hiking and be gone all day without our parents. What more could a kid ask for?''

"I take it some of these other kids your age were of the female variety?'' she asked with a decidedly teasing note in her voice.

"Mmm, yes, you could say that.''

"Ah! Now I understand.''

Trenton's expression sobered. ''Anyway, we were almost home—and let me tell you, driving from Wyoming all the way to central Texas isn't much fun when you have a dad who doesn't like to stop unless it's absolutely necessary. We'd made it to Amarillo when some good old boy decided those twelve beers hadn't impaired his ability to drive a 1952 pickup that hadn't been inspected since it came off the showroom floor. My sister and I were asleep in the back seat. I don't remember anything except waking up in the hospital to find my aunt and uncle there. Bridgette, of course, has no memories of it at all.''

"Trent, I'm so sorry.'' She reached across the table and gave his hand a squeeze.

"Thanks. The years have dulled the pain, but you never forget.''

The arrival of their main courses forced another breather. Melodie found the food delicious, and ate with enthusiasm. She was surprised to find Trenton looking at her approvingly, but she was reluctant to ask why her appetite should please him.

"Anyway—'' Trenton picked up the thread again "—to make a long story short, I understand what you must have felt as a teenager. My aunt and uncle were great, but they had four kids of their own before Bridgette and I got dumped on them. I did my best to be as little trouble as possible. Even though it was never in anything they said or did, I always felt like a burden."

"Bridgette said while you were being the world's perfect kid, she was being the world's biggest brat."

He smiled indulgently. "That's true, but it was a long time ago. She's come far and I'm so proud of her. I don't know what I'd do without her and the kids around."

"You sound more like a proud father than brother and uncle."

"In a lot of ways I do feel more like her father than her brother. I was grown and gone before Bridgette was out of pigtails. And heaven knows I almost think of Joey and Amber as my own. In spirit, I've been the only father they've ever known. I've been baby-sitter, disciplinarian, chauffeur, buddy. And they mean more to me than anything in the world."

Something in Melodie's stomach tightened. She was suddenly sure that Bridgette hadn't discussed Glen's potential job in Chicago with her big brother. Well, Melodie had no intention of spilling the beans.

"They certainly love you. Amber and Joey think you hung the moon," she said quietly.

Trent smiled. "Sometimes I look at them and I think that I can't wait to have my own kids."

That bottom-dropping-out-of-her-stomach feeling was back. Better to pick a safe topic. "Amber certainly is eager for the rehearsal next week."

"What she really can't wait for is that new costume," he said sardonically just before a yawn caught him by surprise. "Excuse me! Must be past my bedtime. Us old folks need our rest."

Melodie patted his arm reassuringly. "Don't worry. I'll help you to the car so you can go night-night."

He gave her a stern look. "Now, don't you start it, too. Bridgette is always making remarks like that."

"Then don't make silly statements about being old. You're not even forty, right?"

"I will be in two months."

"You make it sound like a death sentence, for heaven's sake!"

"No, it's just that I have plans for my life and I'm getting off schedule."

"That's right. Vegetable shopping."

Trent's brow wrinkled in confusion. "I beg your pardon?"

Melodie bit the inside of her cheek. "Nothing."

"Sorry, that was a slip of the tongue I can't let pass."

"It was nothing. Really."

He stared at her, one brow raised questioningly. She felt heat suffuse her face. "It was just something Bridgette said."

"And..."

"And I thought it was funny," she said with a finality she hoped would make him drop it.

"What was funny?"

So much for subliminal persuasion.

"She just said you're bride hunting like most people shop for a head of lettuce."

As she'd feared, his posture went rigid.

"It's true that I'm considering starting a family of my own. However, that doesn't mean I'm preceding as unimaginatively as Bridgette seems to have indicated."

Melodie fought against a laugh. Anytime he got testy, he reverted to that lawyer-type stuffiness she'd noticed when she first met him.

"Really? I got the distinct impression you're interviewing candidates like you would a prospective associate for your firm."

When he winced, she felt bad. She'd meant to tease him, not hit a nerve.

"Whether you want to admit it or not," Trent said, "we all have a set of criteria we use to evaluate the people we let into our lives. Most people make their decisions without knowing how or why they do it."

"With business associates, yes, or choosing a plumber, maybe. But I have a problem with picking a mate quite so...so...dispassionately."

He turned the tables back on her. "I thought you weren't going to get married. You're rather vehement about a subject you're not interested in."

"I wasn't vehement! Besides, we're speaking in general."

"Oh, in general. Right."

"Well, you explain it to me, then. Why are you looking for a wife as if you're searching through a catalog?"

"I'm not searching, per se. I'm merely open to the idea and have a different outlook on my...relationships. Until now, I've been very focused on my career. Now I'm considering that there's room for more in my life."

"Amber and Joey aren't enough?"

"Yes, they are, but they're not my children. And I'm not blind. Bridgette is going to move on and, rightly, she'll be taking the kids with her. It's going to leave a big hole in my life."

His words hit much too close to home for her. It was definitely time to lighten up this conversation.

"Well, good luck in your hunt. I hope you find exactly the right woman for you."

He barked a laugh. "That sounded vaguely like a double entendre."

She shrugged. "I truly didn't mean it to be."

"Don't worry. I'm not insulted. I have a memory of something I read once that went, 'May your life be interesting.' I'm pretty sure it was a curse."

The ensuing lull in the conversation was comfortable, warm, much as the drive over had been. Melodie wasn't used to that. She had been expecting those excruciating silences when she or her date stared at each other and tried to dredge up a new topic to slaughter with feigned laughter. This was nice.

She caught herself up short with a stern reminder that now was not the time to let her guard down. It had been bad enough that she'd let him kiss her at the studio. The last thing she needed was to get cozy with a man who very obviously wanted the wife/kid/picket fence thing. As most of her friends would attest, June Cleaver she was not. Nor was she Harriet Nelson. Heck, she was probably closer to the bumbling but lovable Lucy Ricardo, but even Lucy had wanted that gilded cage. Nope, it was better to enjoy an evening out with Trent, even a lighthearted flirtation, but never to let things progress past that.

"I guess I can see where you got the impression I was stuffy."

She was stunned out of her reverie by Trent's soft-spoken confession. "How's that?"

"I was doing a mental recap of our meetings and I don't think I've acquitted myself all that admirably so far."

She couldn't resist the opening. "You just did it again—talking in thousand-dollar words. It's not that I don't understand you, it's just us normal folk tend to use shorter phrases."

He grinned wryly. "I'll try to remember that."

She nodded. "You do that. Now you've gotten my answer, so it's your turn to explain. You said you misjudged me. How?"

He didn't hesitate. "When I met you at the day-care center, my first thought was that you couldn't possibly be professional enough to be involved in the video."

"Ouch! Don't pull any punches now."

He flushed. "I'm sorry. I didn't mean to insult you, I meant to illustrate what a snob I was being."

"It was the pigs, wasn't it?"

"That and the tie-dye. I have to admit—it was a very...um...eye-catching combination."

"Yeah, you were pretty eye-catching yourself."

"Oh, yeah?" He struggled to hide his pleasure at her compliment.

"Yeah."

"So...do you still think I'm stuffy?"

She had to let out a laugh or she'd burst. "No, Trent, I don't think so anymore. I do like teasing you, though."

"I'm glad."

Maybe the brush of his hand against hers was calculated, maybe an accident. Whichever, his fingers felt warm and wonderful against her arm.

She smiled. "Me, too."

Seven

Trenton watched Melodie with increasing amusement as the evening approached an end. It was somewhat like viewing a witness who starts out assured, and then fades fast as confidence dwindles. The analogy wasn't perfect, of course, but Melodie certainly showed all the signs of someone hiding something. Or of someone who was afraid, and not even sure of what.

If he were doing a rough summation, he would list that while she no longer seemed to think him stuffy, she apparently thought him something akin to an exotic animal—fun to look at but too dangerous to get near. Bridgette the Blabbermouth had obviously filled Melodie's head with images of him madly searching for a bride. While he admitted he was feeling the urge to marry and have children, it didn't mean that he was going to knock the first pretty female who wandered into his path over the head and drag her to his cave to procreate.

Mostly, though, he was curious about this woman, which in itself could prove dangerous. His inability to leave a mystery alone was a foible he acknowledged, and Melodie certainly intrigued him. Her beauty fascinated him as much as the vulnerability she hid under a tough facade. She acted so independent, yet he'd heard with a thirteen-year-old's heart the longing in her voice when she'd spoken of her parents. He'd meant what he said—he knew what it was like to be lonely.

Maybe her nervousness was more easily explained. She could merely be dwelling on the good-night kiss he'd promised earlier. Surely she understood that a healthy dose of sexual attraction didn't mean he was going to drag her to the altar.

"Trent?"

Jerked back to the moment, Trenton was embarrassed to be caught woolgathering.

Melodie nodded toward the woman standing beside the table. "The waitress asked if you wanted anything else."

He hid his chagrin. "Just the check, please." He was surprised his voice sounded nonchalant. At least he hadn't betrayed his responses to the memory of the feel of Melodie's mouth against his, her body pressed between him and the door—

"Trent?" Melodie sounded concerned.

"I'm sorry, Melodie. I don't know what's wrong with me."

She dismissed his apology with a smile and a wave of her hand. "Don't worry about it. But if you don't mind, I'd like to go home now."

"Of course."

With as little fanfare as their arrival, they left. He found it interesting that the closer they came to her house, the more quickly she talked.

"Thank you for dinner, Trent. I didn't realize until I started eating just how hungry I was."

"You're wel—"

"It must be nerves. I was so anxious to see how the group would react to the routine."

"You've made a terrif—"

"The girls were so cute, weren't they? They are so excited about this project. . . ."

Trenton let her babble as he pulled into her driveway and stopped the engine. Unclasping his seat belt, he shifted toward her and put his hand on the back of her seat. The porch light just reached them, casting her beautiful face into soft relief.

". . . moms and dads are so proud. I have to say—"

"Melodie."

She jerked to a stop. "Huh?"

"Has anyone ever told you you talk too much when you're nervous?"

"Well, actually, my friend Serena tells me all the time—"

Her voice squeaked into silence when he slipped his hand to the back of her neck and pulled her gently toward him.

Much as she had at the studio, she seemed frozen. A thought slipped through his mind that she might not be used to men who took the initiative. Her mesmerized expression was innocent, almost confused.

"Melodie, I'm going to kiss you now."

She nodded slowly.

His second taste of her was instantly intoxicating, completely irresistible. Her lips were soft under his, her mouth mobile and pliant. She drew a breath and held it, anticipating him.

He urged her mouth open so he could explore her with his tongue. She tasted of peppermint and chocolate from the candy he'd bought as they'd left the restaurant. Her breath was sweet against his face as she tentatively touched him back, their tongues engaging in a swirling dance of exploration.

It was her hesitation that drew him deeper, urging him to show her that he only wanted to please her, to drive away her reticence and leave room for curiosity. A curiosity that could change to desire.

And he wanted her to desire him. As much as he desired her. No, it was more than want. It was need. A need so powerful it stunned him, not only because it was unexpected, but because it was overwhelming.

Still holding her head in a gentle grip, he used his left hand to begin pulling the pins from her hair.

"Trent—"

"Shhh." He slipped his finger between their nearly touching lips for a moment before returning to his task.

One by one he found the pins that held the heavy weight of her hair. The silken strands cooperated, falling in burnished waves over his wrist as each section was released. He indulged his need to touch her by delving into the molten mass. The sweet scent of her shampoo wafted toward him. It made his body ache in response.

The sound of her soft panting was nearly his undoing, yet still she didn't move. Her hands were clenched into fists on her lap, as though she was holding on for dear life. Maybe she was afraid of herself, of what might happen if she let herself go.

He took his hand from her hair, reluctantly, to stroke her arm. He wanted her to relax, to touch him, explore him.

Shifting in the cramped quarters, he—

Bumped the horn. The short blurt of sound startled them both so badly, they knocked heads.

They sat frozen for a moment. Then Trenton began to laugh. A deep, rumbling, delighted sound that filled the car and urged her to join him.

She couldn't resist. His amusement slipped over her and melted the tension from her shoulders as they laughed until they were breathless again.

Finally he took a breath and rubbed his face with both hands. "I haven't tried to neck in a car in a long, long time."

"Me, either," she said with one last chuckle. "And I have to tell you, I feel a little foolish."

He stroked her chin with his finger. "Please don't. I thought it was nice."

"I did, too. But I still think we're playing with fire."

"It could be fun. To be a little reckless."

"And it could be dangerous."

He cocked his head curiously. "Somehow I haven't pictured you as the overly cautious type. I thought that was my label."

Melodie busied her hands by gathering her hairpins. "Does it really matter?"

"Who gets the label? No, I suppose not. I'm just—"

"I know, I know. Intrigued."

"That. And aroused."

Even in the dim light he could see her blush. Or maybe he simply felt the heat of it from across the car.

"You love doing that to me, don't you?"

"Doing what?" he returned with deliberate innocence.

"Flustering me. Saying something I'm not expecting."

"All right, I confess. I like surprising you. I like not fitting into the role you want to stuff me in. I like taking you off guard. And most of all, I like kissing you."

"Well, yes, but—"

"Admit it, Melodie. You like kissing me, too. You want to know more about me just as much as I want to know more about you."

"Well, yes, but—"

"No buts. You do. I do. So why are we fighting something so simple, so basic?"

"Because I've already told you, sex complicates things."

"And I told you, sex can come later. Why don't you let down your guard and let me in? You might like me."

Melodie became instantly still. She hung her head for a long moment before raising her eyes to his.

"That's just it, Trent. I might like you too much." She swallowed. "And where would that leave me?"

Without a trace of mocking, he answered softly, "Satisfied, I hope."

Clutching her pins and her hip pack to her chest like a shield, she reached for her door handle. "I don't know, Trent. I just don't know. I need some time."

He let her escape out her side of the car but was right beside her as she walked up the path to her porch. He stopped at the screen, having no intention of intruding past that portal this night, but he could not put aside his upbringing and not escort a lady to her house.

He took her keys from her trembling fingers and opened the lock, pushing open the door and giving her back the key ring. He stepped away, but captured her chin to plant a short kiss against her lips.

"I can be amazingly patient when I want to be, Melodie," he said as he retreated toward his car.

"And that's supposed to comfort me?"

An enigmatic shrug was the only answer he'd give her. With a jaunty salute, since he had no hat to tip, he wished her a good-night and left her alone. To dream, he hoped, of him.

He drove away with a contented warmth around his heart. As he passed under a streetlight, his eye caught the glint of something on the seat. Slipping his hand between the pads of leather still warm from her body, he pulled out a pin Melodie had missed.

He lightly scraped his lip with the smooth metal as he drove home. And smiled.

By the end of the next week, Melodie decided that Trenton Laroquette was the master of torture.

Her fingers dug into her pillow as she desperately tried to sleep. Tomorrow was the dress rehearsal and she needed rest or she was going to look like death warmed over on camera.

Just as he'd said he would, he'd given her time and space. The group's schedule had been grueling for the past week, which should have kept her mind occupied. They'd been constantly thrown together as the routines were finished and polished, yet he'd never pressed her, which should have reassured her. Instead, she had come to decide this was more nerve-racking than an all-out assault.

Men! Just when you least expect it, they go and do exactly what you ask them to.

On top of that strain, she hadn't had the luxury of drilling the girls on the exercises. The meetings had been moved to her studio for expediency's sake, so instead of having clean performances ready for the group, as her perfectionistic little heart desired, she had found herself creating and editing on the fly. And in front of an audience. The girls, to their credit, took it all in stride and kept their enthusiasm as they learned each new series.

Now, before she was ready, the moment of truth was upon her. Tomorrow, bright and early, they would be in front of the camera, in living color. Her mind knew it was a dress rehearsal, but her stomach was sure it was the real thing.

She reached behind her and checked her alarm. Again. The last thing she needed to do was oversleep.

Punching her innocent pillow into a more tolerable knot, Melodie tried to relax by going over her mental notes. All the details were covered so she knew she shouldn't worry like this. Then again, *this* hadn't ever had such potential. If the video was successful, for once in her life she could have some breathing space—financially speaking. And she didn't kid herself. The girls were cute, but if she bombed, they all would.

It wasn't helping her anxiety level to add Trent into the equation. Calm Trent. Patient Trent. Unobtrusive Trent.

Irritating, confounding, frustrating Trent.

Never in her life had she felt more off center. And all the while he serenely smiled at her and stayed out of her way.

Somehow she felt herself falling asleep. And fully expected to dream.

Melodie's eyes snapped open. Before she even looked at the clock, she knew something was terribly wrong.

Eight-fifteen! She was supposed to be at the television station at nine. It took forever to dry her hair and the station was near campus—which meant the parking would be abominable. She'd never make it.

Racing through a shower, she dressed in record time. Her hair left a wet streak down the back of her leotard, but it would dry. Grabbing a brush and her makeup, she dashed out of the house and was on her way by quarter 'til.

She couldn't believe it. She'd checked her clock six or seven times before she'd fallen asleep. As she cursed softly while begging her car to start, a vague memory surfaced of the alarm going off and of herself reaching for the snooze button. Maybe she'd accidentally turned it off....

It was a moot point now. She was on her way, but even if all the traffic gods smiled on her, she would still be late. And Trent would be thoroughly perturbed with her. If she was sure of one thing, he would win the Mr. Punctual Award hands down. Just as she would win the Miss She'll-Be-Late-For-Her-Own-Funeral Award.

If there were ever two more incompatible people than herself and Trent, she couldn't think of them. He was early, she was late. He liked pasta primavera, she liked pizza. He liked walks in the park, she liked long bubble baths. He said tomato, she said—

Oh, stop it.

Suffice it to say that as soon as this rehearsal was over and she had two free seconds, she was going to tell Trent to get out of her head and out of her life. Yes, he was sexier than any man she'd ever seen. Yes, she wanted to be with him more than anything she'd ever wanted. And just as much, she knew it would spell disaster if she indulged in this wanton desire.

She was too caught up in him already, prior to any real goings-on, to even imagine what shape she'd be in if she succumbed to him. None of the men in her life had affected her this way presex, or even postsex. Admittedly, Serena seemed to think the list was much longer than it actually was, but the fact remained that the few men who had made the jump from friend to lover had never twisted her into a mass of knots.

So give Trent a trophy for doing it without even trying. God help her if he put real effort into it.

At the first shudder of her car underneath her, Melodie told herself not to panic. She was on MoPac, a busy thoroughfare at any time of day, and there were call boxes. If worse came to worst, there were neighborhoods off every exit.

At the second shudder, mild alarm set in.

At the third shudder, dread took hold.

At the fourth and final shudder, followed by a pathetic cough, Melodie eased the dying vehicle onto the shoulder and let hysteria begin.

Resting her head on her steering wheel, she fought a battle between tears of self-pity and insane laughter.

She nearly jumped out of her skin when a shadow came over her and a deep voice said, "Can I help you, ma'am?"

A nice-looking man in a charcoal gray suit was hunched over, looking at her through her open window. A quick glance in her rearview mirror showed a convertible sports car a few feet behind her.

"Um, do you have a car phone?"

"Yes, I do. Would you like me to call a wrecker? Or could I take you somewhere?"

"No, actually, I need to call a friend before I do anything. Would you mind?"

"Not at all."

The gentleman handed her his phone as she stood beside his car and explained that he'd been behind her when he'd seen her slowing. He said he hoped he hadn't scared her. She assured him that he hadn't, and expressed her appreciation as she listened to ring after ring. Finally a voice came on announcing the studio and advising her to pick from the following menu or wait for an operator. Since most cellulars didn't have tones to activate the nuisance of automated systems, she smiled apologetically and waited for an infernal operator.

The timing beep reminded her several times that she was racking up minutes, but at that point, she didn't know what else to do. By the time the operator had put her through and Trent came on the line, she was about to start biting her nails.

"Melodie? Where are you?"

"Broken down on MoPac. Just before the Thirty-fifth Street exit. A nice man stopped and let me use his car phone."

"Are you all right? Do I need to call the police?" Trent's voice sounded strained.

"No, I'm fine. I'm just going to be really late."

"Get in your car and lock the doors. I'll be there in ten minutes."

"Trent—"

"For once, Melodie, please don't argue with me."

"All right."

She ended the call and smiled at the polite gentleman. "Thank you so much. My friend is on his way."

After she refused his offer to wait with her, the man reluctantly drove away. All she could think about was how often she'd read about situations like this that turned out gruesome. In her case, she'd been lucky that a guy a whole lot like Trent had stopped to offer her aid.

It wasn't that she needed a Prince Charming—she punched the steering wheel—for her dragon had slayed itself. But just this once, she was going to relax and let someone help her without her feeling as if she were a failure. After all, Sir Trenton was the one who had ordered her to sit still. If he was going to be autocratic, he should expect to be treated accordingly.

She smiled sheepishly, despite the fact that she was alone, and warned herself to be prepared for Sir Trenton to be just the tiniest bit put out with her, even if this wasn't her fault. Technically. That was the problem with knights—she doubted they dwelled much on technicalities.

As she worried, his roaring steed pulled to a stop behind her.

Melodie jerked the cotton sundress off over her head and threw it onto the pile of clothes on the bed.

The rehearsal had gone beautifully—she should be euphoric.

She wasn't.

She hated being beholden to anyone. Despite her pep talk as she'd waited for Trent to arrive, she couldn't help a sense of obligation to him for having her car towed. He hadn't even yelled at her, which made her feel even more guilty. In fact, he'd been so worried about her safety, she'd apologized for not being scared!

She hated feeling awkward for being late and putting everyone off schedule. And she hated this sense of duty to Bridgette to show up for dinner and dancing to celebrate. She didn't want to celebrate. She was being petulant and moody and she wanted to be left alone. Or rather, she wanted to say what she needed to say to Trent and then be left alone.

She was almost sorry the rehearsal had been such a roaring success. The children had behaved so well, and each take had gone increasingly better so that they had finished right on time. She almost wished it had been a disaster so everyone would have gone home.

The sweat hadn't dried on her forehead before Bridgette had announced that they needed to party. She'd said their hard work had left nothing to do but show up Monday for the final filming, so tonight was perfect for the adults to go out to dinner and do some dancing themselves. Melodie grimaced at the memory, but she hadn't had the heart to be a wet rag. This was Bridgette's moment to shine.

On the other hand, Melodie reminded herself, if she'd been a little quicker or a little more forceful, she wouldn't now be standing in front of her closet in her bra and panty hose, trying on every piece of clothing she owned while *he* sat channel surfing in her living room.

But the truth of it all was, she was the most perturbed with herself for working herself into a tizzy trying to find just the right dress that would make her look beautiful to Trent. No matter how many times she told herself it shouldn't matter if Trent thought she looked beautiful, she kept vetoing outfits.

Squaring her shoulders, she went back to the beige palazzo pants and sleeveless tunic, holding them against her as she stood in front of the mirror. Comfortable, cool, casual. Not too daring, yet provocative.

With a gusty sigh, she tossed them back on the bed.

Not right for dancing. She needed something with a full skirt. She loved the feel of yards of silky fabric swishing around her legs as she moved.

Determined to get this over with, she reached in and grabbed a floral-print shirtwaist that had the requisite full skirt. An oversize belt emphasized her waist, and gathered, short sleeves gave her plenty of room for turns and maneuvering. She forced herself over to her dresser and chose accenting jewelry before she changed her mind again. She stopped just long enough to grab her comfortable blue pumps and her prettiest lace shawl before hurrying to the living room.

She stopped short in the doorway, her shoes hanging on the tips of her fingers. The man was asleep! She'd been hurrying so fast she felt as though she'd run a marathon. And for what?

Her disgruntlement faded as she moved closer and looked at him. In repose, Trent seemed as if he hadn't been getting any more rest than she had these past few days. Why hadn't she noticed the shadows under his eyes before now? Or the little tension lines on his forehead that weren't completely erased, even in his sleep?

Was that her fault? She hoped not, yet at the same time, a part of her was glad that he was as affected by her as she was by him. It was only fair that she not be the only one tossing and turning all night.

The longer she watched him, the more drawn she felt to him. God help her, she knew it was wrong, but she couldn't stop herself. As if driven by an outside force, she leaned over to brush back the lock of hair that had fallen forward over his forehead.

He smiled as he opened his eyes. "What a nice surprise."

She flushed and cursed her fair complexion. "I...um...don't know why I did that. I'm sorry."

She tried to draw away, but he caught her arm.

"Don't be. I could never be sorry that you touched me."

Despite his protest, she pulled her arm from his grip and retreated to the dining room. She fiddled with transferring her ID and money to her purse from her pouch. He stood a respectful two chairs down.

"You look incredible," he complimented her softly, almost as though afraid he'd startle her.

She couldn't stop the hot rush of pleasure at the sincerity in his voice. The sensation intensified when she looked up from her task and saw the heat in his eyes. "Thank you," she managed in a normal voice, but his admiration and her reaction only served to remind her that it was imperative she set the ground rules.

"Trent, we need to talk about tonight."

He waited expectantly. She cleared her throat.

"I've been doing a lot of thinking, and I want you to know I'm really flattered by your interest. . . ."

"But," he supplied helpfully.

"But I don't think we should pursue this any further. In fact, I wouldn't even be going tonight if this weren't so important to Bridgette."

"I thought you looked rather like a fox cornered by hounds this afternoon."

She grimaced. "Was I that obvious?"

"Only to me."

She studied her hands for a moment. "You've been true to your word about giving me time. And I appreciate it, but I think after tonight we shouldn't see each other anymore."

"We'll see each other at the final shoot."

She gave him an exasperated look. "You know what I mean."

Pulling a chair out, he turned it around with a twist of his wrist and straddled the cushioned seat. Folding his arms across the top, he laid his chin on his hands.

"No, actually, I don't know what you mean. We haven't *seen* each other at all yet, in the strictest sense, so how can we stop what hasn't even started?"

"We went out to dinner—"

"Which you were quite insistent was not a date."

"Yes, but—"

"I, on the other hand, feel that it is only right, in the interest of fairness, that we *see* each other at least once before making any determinations."

"I don't—"

"I tell you what. Why don't we take advantage of tonight? If you promise me that you'll let go of the panic button and just spend this evening with me of your own free will, afterward I'll accept whatever your decision may be.''

''Trent, I—''

''Come on, Melodie.'' He dismounted and moved in front of her, holding out his hands. ''Trust me. Take the chance.''

His heart beat loudly in the quiet of the house. The clock on the wall ticked off the seconds. He held his breath. He knew she was weakening, that she was fighting herself, and that gave him hope. Hope that she would let her guard down just this once, or rather, just with him.

And then she put her hands in his.

Eight

Melodie closed her eyes and laid her head against Trent's shoulder as the band played a slow, dreamy tune. She and Trent had cut quite a rug over the course of the evening. She had forgotten how wonderful it was to dance with a man who knew how to lead. Once men learned she was a professional, it seemed the most confident of them became intimidated and she found herself leading backwards more often than not.

But Trent, not surprisingly, was as in control on the dance floor as he probably was in the courtroom. Before the last waltz, she'd been twirled and dipped and sambaed and jitterbugged by a master. She was thoroughly impressed and having the time of her life.

It was as if Trent's entreaty had given her tacit permission to suspend judgment for this one evening. She couldn't think of another occasion when she'd been able to push her reservations and anxieties aside so

completely as she had tonight. And she was determined to keep it up. If tonight was a moment stolen
out of time, so be it. She would enjoy it to the fullest
and place these memories in a special corner of her
mind.

"Stop it," Trent whispered against her hair.

"Stop what?" she asked dreamily.

"Thinking."

"How did you know I was thinking?"

"I could feel you."

She giggled. "You should be feeling a lot of me right
about now."

Trent used a tight, inside turn to pull her even closer.
"Yes, but not nearly enough."

She rubbed her cheek against his shoulder, and she
resisted the urge to check if her feet were still on the
floor.

The song ended and they paused with the musicians, waiting until the music picked up again in a slow
waltz. The change in positions, calling for a firmer
arm, gave her the chance to look up.

"You're very good at this," she said, smiling. "I'm
impressed."

"Thank you."

That was another thing she liked about Trent. He
could take a compliment.

As they whirled to take the corner, her dress fan-
ning out and around her legs, Melodic giggled again.
Since she wasn't usually the giggling type, it surprised
her.

"What's funny?" he asked.

"Not funny. Fun. I think I love waltzing more than
any other rhythm. If I have the right partner, that is.
It's such a sensuous dance."

"See, I told you there was a romantic hidden beneath that exterior."

"I've never denied being a romantic. I'm just a practical romantic."

"That's an oxymoron."

"For some people, maybe. I reserve the right to be unique."

He smiled and took her out of the path of a rather energetic elderly man and his partner, then they rejoined the fluid stream.

"I want you, you know."

He said the words as matter-of-factly as if he were warning her he was going to change their dance pattern. Or inquiring if she wanted some refreshment. Or pointing out that she had a run in her stocking.

Her throat went dry. Then the trembling started in her fingers. If he hadn't been clasping her hand firmly, she was sure it would have wriggled right out of his grip.

Yes, she knew he wanted her. But she thought the rule was that all moves were to be made subtly. Announcing his desire was not subtle. It left her no maneuvering room, no chance to misdirect, to pretend to misunderstand, to move the field of play laterally rather than forward or backward.

The problem was, her offensive coordinator—her heart—was screaming, "Go! Go!" On the other hand, the defensive or "head" coach was yelling, "Time out!"

Her impulsive side wanted to jump in with both feet while her wounded side was holding on to the dock with arms strengthened by panic.

Good Lord, she was mixing her metaphors. Or were they analogies? Just one more sign she was at the edge. . . .

For the moment, she chose to pretend she hadn't heard him and kept waltzing, ignoring the misstep that had surely given her away. At least he was too much of a gentleman to call attention to her inelegance.

He remained the perfect date as they rejoined the group at the table, and throughout the rest of the evening. He courteously granted Glen leave to take her around the floor, and even Juan and Ronald asked for turns, although none of the men left Bridgette and Cassie idle. Her spirits were soaring again by the time the evening waned and everyone said their goodbyes.

She shivered deliciously when Trent traced her shoulders with gentle fingers as he draped her shawl around her and guided her through the darkness to his car.

The street lamps bathed them in intermittent light as they drove away in comfortable silence.

He broke the quiet when he glanced her way and asked, "Can I talk you into joining me for a midnight swim? I couldn't stand it if the evening ended yet."

"It's been wonderful," she agreed, "but I hardly thought ahead to bring a suit with me."

"You can use one of the ones Bridgette leaves at the house."

Her smile was surprisingly content. "Okay."

He gave her a startled glance. "That's it? Okay?"

"Isn't that what you wanted to hear?"

"Yes, but I was sure I was going to have to put up a harder fight."

She chuckled. "I can argue with you if you want me to."

"Oh, no. That's fine. You just caught me off guard."

"Good. You were getting a little too smug for my taste."

He smiled back at her. "I'm never smug."

Since he was watching the road, as he was supposed to, he missed the roll of her eyes.

Miles traveled under the tires. She waited until they had reached his house and he was escorting her up the back walkway before she spoke again.

"We're going to have sex, aren't we." It was a statement, not a question.

Her abruptness earned her another surprised glance, and he stopped in his tracks.

He looked at her for a long moment before answering, "I was rather hoping we'd make love."

"Semantics," she said with a shrug, and turned to continue walking.

"Like hell it is!"

His vehemence startled her, as well as his touch when he took her arm and whirled her to face him.

"I've had sex, Melodie, and I've made love. There's a world of difference. I think you know that."

She shrugged again.

"I'm very clear that I want to make love with you, so if sex is all you're after, we can enjoy a nice swim and I'll take you home. I want more than two bodies jumping into bed, Melodie. I want a whole lot more."

"What about what I want?"

"Don't you get it? This *is* about what you want. You call the shots about what happens tonight, but if you decide to stay with me, I'm going to touch and taste and love every inch of your body." He unlocked the door and ushered her inside. "When I'm done, there will be no question as to whether we've merely had sex, or something much more."

Tears pooled in her eyes, but she refused to acknowledge them. Had it really been that long since she'd been with a man? Since she'd had someone who cared about her, what she wanted, her pleasure? If her reaction was any indication, obviously so. Maybe she'd been testing him on a subconscious level. Or maybe she was dangerously close to trawling the final mortar onto the brick wall she'd been building around her heart, letting her body respond as nature would require, but keeping her soul remote.

And he was right. Again. She'd had sex, too. And made love. And she was well aware what the differences were. Not that a little down-and-dirty sex was a bad thing, every now and then. But she knew that it should be the exception, not the rule.

She bolstered her flagging spirits by reminding herself that he was also right on another point—that she was calling the shots. He might be the one with abundant self-confidence, but she was making the rules here. If she chose to claim this one night with him, then she was doing so with her eyes wide open. No morning-after tears or recriminations. If this was what she wanted, then fine. If not, that was fine, too.

She had no illusions that he was professing his undying love or that he would go down on his knee and ask her to marry him. After all, that was the last thing she wanted, she assured herself. If anything, she was still being consistent in choosing a man who was no threat to her freedom. Trent was looking for a wife in the near future, and since she had no intention of giving up her dreams or her career for any man, no matter how gorgeous, this interlude with Trent could be fun and mutually satisfying. And when it was over, she could say goodbye with a little sadness, but no devastation. What more could she ask?

Trent had been leading her through the house as she'd been lost in her thoughts. She tugged on his hand lightly and brought him to a stop.

"Trent, I've changed my mind."

She saw a look of sadness, of regret, sweep across his face.

"It's all right. I understand. Let's go back out the way we came and I'll reset the alarm."

She shook her head. "You don't understand. I wasn't asking to leave, I just don't want to go for a swim."

He frowned in confusion. "You don't?"

"No, I've decided I'd rather make love."

A slow smile lit his face.

"This way, then, my lady," he said, taking her hand again and heading down the long hall she'd toured the first time she'd been here. Only, on her previous visits, she hadn't seen his bedroom.

With a flip of a switch, he turned on the lamps that graced the polished wood nightstands. She looked at the king-size bed and felt a delicious shiver. Above the headboard were three mirrored panes, each framed in the same dark cherry wood. Recessed lights reflected softly into the room.

As she watched in the mirror, Trent moved behind her, winding his arms around her waist to pull her against him. Slipping the collar of her dress down, he nuzzled against the back of her ear and a tremor seized her.

Melodie covered her hands with his and leaned into the hard plane of his chest. Stretching her neck, she willingly gave him more room to explore.

She hardly noticed as he loosened the buttons of her dress one by one and slid the garment off her arms, pushing it down until it hung around her waist by the elastic band. She was too busy concentrating on the sensation of Trent's tongue tracing the taut muscle from her ear to her shoulder and watching his dark head in the mirror.

When she would have faced him, he stopped her. As he had once before, his fingers unerringly found the pins holding up the mass of her hair and worked until the entire weight came tumbling down. She sighed as he fanned his fingers through the rippling strands and combed out the length.

Again, when she tried to turn, he put his hands on her shoulders and kept her steady.

"Don't be in such a hurry," he whispered against her ear. "We have all night."

"But I want to touch you," she said in a husky plea.

His deep chuckle rippled through her. "And I want you to. But not yet."

His hands slid along the silk of her skin to cup her breasts and she found she couldn't breathe. Instinctively she arched farther back against him and pressed into his firm massage.

She almost wept when he stopped, only to have anticipation sweep through her as she watched the mirror, fascinated, as his fingers deftly undid the front hook of her bra and slowly peeled the lacy creation away from her body.

His eyes met hers in the glass as he cupped the weight of her in his hands again, tracing her rigid nipples with his fingertips.

"You're driving me insane," she gasped raggedly.

"I hope so. It's only fair," he answered against her throat, his voice as rough as hers.

He finally let her turn. He framed her face with tender hands before wrapping his arms around her to crush her against him.

His mouth claimed hers. The gentle teasing was gone, replaced by a grinding passion that threatened to bruise them both. Melodie didn't care. All she wanted was to get closer, and closer still.

She forced her hands between them, her fingers clumsy as she tried to unbutton his shirt. She couldn't tear her mouth away from his to see what she was doing. When she finally exposed the hot expanse of skin, she crushed her breasts against him, burying her nipples in the crisp, silky hairs that covered his chest. She shifted against the rigid evidence of his desire, pressing herself more completely against his length.

All the while his lips explored hers. His tongue delved into her mouth. She sucked him deeper, and was rewarded with a low-pitched moan.

His insistence that they take time became lost in a flurry of motion as they stripped away the clothing that kept them apart. Taking her with him, he moved to the bed and swept away the comforter to lay her on cool, soft sheets that smelled like sunshine.

The air-conditioning made the house decadently cool, but it wasn't the cold air that made her quake.

It was the passion blazing in Trent's eyes.

He stretched out beside her, claiming her breast again. She explored his form, as well, tracing the shape of his muscular chest, burrowing her fingers in his wiry curls, lightly scraping her nails across his strong, square jaw and raking down his short, dark hair.

Every movement was urgent, filled with desire. An aching, demanding desire that felt unquenchable.

His hands left her torso to stroke as far as he could reach down her hips, along her thighs and back up again. With each brush, his fingers grazed the center of her desire, making her jump at the brief intimacy but leaving her hungry for more. She moved restlessly on the bed.

She mimicked his sensual teasing, making him jolt and moan as she closed her fingers around his smooth, hot length.

"Oh, Melodie," he choked, closing his eyes against the sensation. He dropped his forehead onto her shoulder, his breathing harsh and ragged.

"What?" she asked, startled, suddenly uncertain.

He kissed the creamy white expanse of her skin and shook his head. "I'm sorry. I've got to slow down or I'm going to ruin this."

The moment of trepidation evaporated. In its place came a sweet warmth as she heard the fear in his voice, his concern for her.

"But I don't want you to stop," she assured him, as she traced him with her fingernail.

His hand trembled as he stroked up her thigh to find her hot and wet, waiting for him impatiently. She rocked against his fingers as he rubbed against her aching center.

In one beautifully fluid motion he moved over her and between her thighs. In the next, he slid slowly into her. Melodie refused to breathe, refused to do anything that would take away from the sensation of him filling her, of her body molding to accept him completely.

She gasped as he withdrew, only to release her breath in a shudder when he slipped inside again. And again. And again. Until her world consisted only of the feeling of his body melded with hers.

Her response was inexorable, a tide building with each thrust of his hips, until the sensations burst forth, forcing a gasp from her lips.

"Oh, Trent," she cried as she exploded into a thousand pieces.

His mouth fused to hers as he joined her in release.

The room was filled with the sound of their rapid breaths, the scent of their passion and the stillness of the night.

Trent held his weight off her and looked down. His expression was unlike any she had ever seen—dark, intense, indefinable.

"You are so beautiful," he whispered, dropping a kiss onto her sweaty brow.

Slowly he extricated himself and lay beside her once more. She was amazed at how bereft she felt without his weight pressing against her.

She wasn't aware she'd made a mew of disappointment until he tilted her face toward him.

"We're not done," he assured her with a thoroughly male smile. "That just took the edge off."

She answered with a smile of her own and shifted so that she was the aggressor this time, claiming his lips in a kiss that conveyed the depth of her still-warm desire. In a graceful movement mimicking his, she straddled his hips so she could massage his chest and arms. His hands rested on her thighs, stroking the

rounded pads of her buttocks as she rocked forward
and back in her play.

"I like touching you," she confessed, using the edge
of the soft sheet to wipe his forehead.

"Be my guest," he urged, spreading his arms wide
in invitation.

She indulged herself, learning the shape of every
muscle, teasing him about the gray hairs she found
among the field of black and enjoying the sensations
aroused by watching him watch her.

"Tell me what you want," she said, wriggling down
until their bodies were intimately snuggled together
and her head rested on his chest.

Trent traced her spine with his knuckles and made
her quiver against him. "I want to go sit in the hot tub
for a while, have a glass of wine and come back in here
and play some more."

She lifted her head to look at him. "In that order?" she teased.

"Well, we can get the wine first."

With a strength that surprised and pleased her, he
sat up with her still on his lap. The shift in positions
thrust her breasts forward and he nuzzled them lav-
ishly. With one final sucking kiss, he stood, holding
her close until she had her legs underneath her.

She grabbed Trent's shirt from the floor and threw
it on, fastening the bottom few buttons and rolling up
the too-long sleeves until her hand appeared. Trent
slipped on a robe but left it unbelted as he weaved his
fingers with hers and led the way to the kitchen.

Melodie was amazed at her lack of embarrassment.
He looked sexy as hell in his partial concealment, and
if his smoldering glances were any indication, she
didn't look half-bad in her mostly open shirt.

"Blush or burgundy?" he asked, showing her two bottles he had chilled in the refrigerator.

She chose the blush, and retrieved two wineglasses when he asked. Trent was soon leading the way to the hot tub, a bucket of ice and bottle of chilled wine in his arm, his other hand firmly holding hers.

Gas lights ringing the deck cast a soft glow over the water of both the pool and the tub. The moon was full, casting long shadows behind them as they walked across the decking. Giant trees and privacy fencing assured their seclusion.

As she glanced around his miniature Garden of Eden, it seemed the most natural thing in the world to drop her shirt and slip naked into the gurgling water with him.

Gliding through the effervescence to Trent, she straddled his lap and entwined her arms around his neck. Their kisses were as long and slow as the previous ones had been torrid. They lost track of time as the heat and wine relaxed them. They indulged in their languid love play until the burning touches under the blanket of bubbles rekindled their excitement to a raging flame.

Trent surprised her when his strong arms lifted her out of the water and balanced her on the edge of the hot tub. She barely had time to exclaim, "Oh!" before she felt his hands part her thighs and his mouth began to tease her, to please her as his tongue aroused a maelstrom of need.

She clung to his shoulders as her head fell back and wave after wave of pleasure so exquisite she could not contain it drove over her, through her, leaving her wanton as she lost all inhibition, dropped her knees farther apart and begged him to give her the release just waiting on the edges of her sanity.

When he finally did as she bade him, her cries echoed off the plate-glass doors as she fell from heaven back to earth.

Trenton propped his head on his hand as he watched Melodie sleep. The woman was a sexual dynamo, there was no doubt. The gift of her response in the hot tub had made his body answer with equal urgency. She'd turned the tables on him in the shower, giving back to him a pleasure that had nearly driven him to his knees.

She had hardly given him time to recover when they'd reached the bed again before she had poured her passion on him once more. Finally, exhausted but replete beyond anything he'd ever known, they'd fallen into an exhausted slumber, entwined in each other's arms.

Now he stared at her in the moonlight that bathed her in a pale glow. It made her seem ethereal, angelic, a creature untouchable by the pagan passion that had held him enraptured just a short while ago.

A smile curved Trent's lips. My, but he tended to get fanciful in the depths of the night. Must be all that classical literature he'd read in college.

He had expected it to be wonderful. And it had been more, much more than the word could convey. He just hadn't expected it to change his life.

Melodie awoke to find morning sunlight streaming across the bed. She stretched and snuggled under the covers again—

And sat bolt upright with the sheet clutched against her.

God, she hated mornings after. Which was probably the reason she'd had so few of them.

She wondered where Trent was and hoped he wouldn't make this any more difficult than it had to be.

Last night had been the most incredible sex she had ever had and it would be a memory she would cherish forever. She was sure to dream of this experience for years to come. Maybe it would keep her company on some lonely evenings in the future.

Now if she could just get dressed, greet Trent casually and get home before a scene ruined everything, she'd count the evening a success.

Melodie pulled her dress from the arm of the chair in front of the fireplace. It was a shame it was summer—she'd never made love in front of a fireplace in a bedroom before. Her fingers fumbled as she caught Trent's shirt before it fell to the floor. Without thinking, she brought the now-wrinkled cotton up to her nose and inhaled the spicy, male scent that clung to the material.

When she realized what she was doing, she threw the shirt back onto the chair as though it burned her.

"Enough of that nonsense," she scolded herself as she jerked on her underwear and panty hose. Her dress quickly followed, then her belt and jewelry until once again she was dressed as she had been last night.

A quick search through her purse located her brush, and after a few brisk strokes, she plaited her hair and let it hang casually over her shoulder.

There. Back to normal.

She snapped her purse shut and slung the strap over her shoulder. She looked up to head for the door—

But the sight of Trent stopped her in her tracks.

Nine

One look at his face and she knew she was a fool.

She'd thought she could make love with him, be with him as she'd never been with another man and then walk away with casual calm.

She was a fool.

If she hadn't seen him, she would probably have been all right. And certainly if she hadn't seen him bearing breakfast on a bed tray with pink flowers in a white vase off to the side. Nobody had ever brought her breakfast in bed. Nobody. Just as nobody had perched her on the side of a hot tub and . . .

She shook her head.

Trent finally moved from his frozen stance in the doorway and placed the tray on the corner of the bed. He turned around with his hands buried in the pockets of his robe.

"I take it you're not hungry."

"Um, no, but thank you. That was sweet."

His smile didn't quite meet his eyes. "Sweet. Hmm."

She twisted the strap of her purse around her fingers and looked away from Trent. She didn't want to admit she'd seen hurt in his eyes—something much deeper than mere disappointment—when he'd taken in her appearance.

"Going so soon?"

She closed her eyes against sudden tears. "Trent, please. Don't act so . . . so—"

"So casual? I might point out that I'm not the one who jumped out of bed and got ready to leave as though the house were on fire. What were you going to do? Slip out the door without so much as a note?"

"Trent, please—"

"You've already said that. Let's try something else."

She swallowed. The hurt was gone from his face. In its place was an anger that was almost palpable.

"Look, this is the very reason I'm going to leave. I don't do mornings after with much grace so I avoid them. I never intended to stay the whole night."

He let the silence linger.

"Yes, well . . ." She took several steps toward the door as carefully as if skirting a lion. "I'll just call a cab and head home—"

"Over my dead body."

She halted at the door. "I beg your pardon?"

"If you're so damned determined to get home, I'll take you. Give me a minute to get into some jeans."

"That's not necessary. Really—"

"No. It's necessary. Really."

The ride to her house took place in interminable silence. In her driveway once again, she turned to him.

"Trent, I know I've insulted you and I'm truly sorry."

After a second, he turned his gaze from straight ahead to bore into her. "What did I do wrong, Melodie?"

She closed her eyes and pressed her hands against the ache in her stomach. "You didn't do anything wrong. Last night was truly incredible. But I meant what I said. Mornings after are simply hell. Everyone wants to make more of it than there is."

"Make more of it than there is," he repeated softly. "I take that to indicate that last night was simply a pleasant interlude to be forgotten now that 'it' is over."

"No, I won't forget last night. Ever. But you have to admit it was a mistake."

His knuckles went white around the steering wheel. "I don't have to admit anything of the kind. And if you can convince yourself of that lie, you're a better person than I am."

"Trent, in my living room you stood there and promised me before we went dancing that you'd accept my decision. Well, I decided to have se—"

One look at his eyes and she immediately amended her statement.

"I decided to make love with you. And it was wonderful. But it's over, and we have to get back to the business at hand."

"Ah. The business."

Now she was starting to get mad.

"Yes, the business. I told you, several times if I remember, that business and sex don't mix. This certainly proves me right."

"All this proves is that you're a coward, Melodie."

She jerked back as though slapped. Her jaw worked for several seconds before she finally said, "You can believe whatever you'd like. Until this project is finished, I believe it would be best if we saw as little of each other as possible."

The passenger door slammed. Trenton rested his head on his hands for a moment before jerking his door open, and he called out to Melodie from across the yard.

"I can't let it end like this, Melodie."

Melodie ran back across the yard. "Do you mind! I don't think all of the people in Tarrytown heard you!"

He ignored her gibe but lowered his voice. "I can't let you just walk away like this. I thought I could. I thought I was mad enough, but I was wrong." Trent scrubbed his hands through his hair. "Damn it, Melodie, I can't just treat what happened last night like some casual, one-night stand." He grabbed her by the shoulders and forced her to look at him. "Except one night with you changed my life."

Her lip trembled, but she forced it under control. "I'm glad last night was special to you. It was special to me, too, but we have different agendas for our lives, Trent. I'm not going to get involved in an ongoing relationship with you. It would destroy me."

"What do you mean—"

Her shoulders wilted, despite her attempt to stay strong. Any second now she was going to collapse, and she wanted to do it in the privacy of her own home.

"No, Trent, not now. I just can't talk about it anymore. Please. Go."

Her eyes begged him to believe her. When he got back into the car, she nearly lost the last remnants of her control. Only by sheer will did she stay upright.

"All right, Melodie. I'll go. But this isn't over."

She nodded, not necessarily in agreement, but because she would have done just about anything to end the standoff.

"I'll call you later."

She paused at his words, but didn't turn around. Then she simply put one foot in front of the other until she reached her porch and let herself inside the house.

She made it all the way to the couch before the tears blinded her completely.

Trent waited until late the next morning to call Melodie, on the assumption that her night had been as restless as his. But unlike him, maybe she'd been able to sleep in.

"Happy Fourth of July," he answered her greeting.

"It's the Fourth? Already?"

He heard incredulity in her voice. "I know, it's hard to believe. But it's refreshing to know I'm not the only one oblivious to the time."

Her strained laugh tugged at his heart.

He struggled for words in the ensuing silence. "Melodie, you all right?"

"I'm . . . okay. You?"

"Yeah, me, too. Listen, among other things, I'm calling about tonight."

"Tonight?"

He paused. "Fireworks on Town Lake? Bridgette and Glen needed some time alone so we promised we'd take Amber and Joey, remember?"

"I'd forgotten." She sighed.

"I'm glad I called, then."

"I'm not." Her tone was teasing and serious at the same time. "Now I have to figure a way to weasel out of this."

He waited. "Are you serious?"

Her forced chuckle reassured him.

"No, I think we've played that game already. I made a commitment to Amber and Joey, and I won't disappoint them."

To say he was surprised would have been simplistic. He had been absolutely sure she would back out of the evening. It was all too easy to recall her face when he'd pulled out of her driveway yesterday morning, a morning he had expected to be filled with the afterglow of their lovemaking. Instead, the vision of her taut features and posture would probably haunt him for a long time.

"Can I pick you up at six? Amber is beside herself to have a real picnic. We'll take a blanket and a cooler so we can grab a choice spot."

"That's probably a good idea. The traffic is always horrible. I'll see you at six, then."

Trent replaced the receiver slowly after they said their goodbyes. He wasn't foolish—he knew the evening could turn out tense. But since he also knew that Melodie would avoid him completely if given the chance, he felt justified for taking advantage of the holiday. He was hoping the festive atmosphere, the outdoors and being effectively chaperoned would give

Melodie enough comfort to relax and open the door for them to talk later.

The phone rang, startling him. For a moment, he worried that it was Melodie calling back to change her mind.

"Trenton? It's Erin McDonnell. We met at the fund-raiser for the Austin Young Women Lawyers' Association last month?"

"Oh, yes, how are you?" A picture came to his mind of a tall, elegantly suited blonde with a glass of white wine in her hand. She was an up-and-coming junior partner with one of the biggest firms in town. She already had a reputation, a damn good one in fact. He'd found her witty and intelligent, on top of the fact that she was talented and quite beautiful. She was exactly the kind of woman who met all of his criteria.

"Listen, a few of us have rented a party boat and are going to cruise up the lake this evening. You know, have our own little Fourth of July party? I'd love it if you'd join us."

Not too long ago, he would have said yes if she'd asked him before he'd made a promise to Joey and Amber. After all, intimate gatherings like that were the perfect chances for stage two—the getting-to-know-you part—with a prospective candidate. Yet, when he considered it, he wasn't even disappointed at the missed opportunity.

How odd.

He found it interesting that upon meeting Erin, he'd immediately tagged her as someone he could get serious about. She had certainly given him every sign that she was available in an open, up-front way that lacked any of the coy maneuverings he despised.

But all he could do, as he thanked Erin and declined the invitation, was compare her to a woman who shopped at street corner bazaars and taught the hokey-pokey to four-year-olds. And Erin was the one who came up lacking.

Melodie was on pins and needles by the time Trent pulled into her driveway. She was waiting on the porch with a plastic plate of lemon bars as her contribution to the picnic fare. Trent hadn't said to bring anything, but she didn't want to come empty-handed. She would be embarrassed if anyone had seen her near panic in having to decide between these and home-made chocolate-chip cookies. She'd nearly worried herself into a tizzy before deciding the heat would make chocolate a bad choice.

Joey was quite the gentleman as he gave up the coveted front seat. Amber chatted ceaselessly from the moment they left the driveway until they spread their blanket on the patch of grass they claimed for the evening. This was the first time she'd been allowed to stay up for the show, and the only thing that put a stop to her stream of questions and comments was a mouthful of fried chicken.

Melodie glanced over her shoulder to watch the musicians arriving and making their way to the side of the auditorium. The grassy tiers of the shores of Town Lake were across the street from the huge speakers being erected, but Trent had picked a perfect spot to hear the Austin Symphony before the fireworks began. The show always impressed her, but she had the distinct feeling she wouldn't be quite as focused this year. Not with two adorable children distracting her, and one very potent man demanding her attention without even trying.

Luckily the children kept the mood too light for Melodie to feel awkward. Trent played catch with Joey in the still-powerful sunlight, and Melodie helped Amber dress her dolls. Her concentration was not on the fashion show, though. Her gaze kept slipping to the boys, especially when their laughter carried to her on the warm breeze.

The area quickly became crowded with blankets and lawn chairs, coolers and picnic baskets. The boys gave up their game and wove their way through the patchwork of people to their spot. When they all finally settled to await the show, Melodie leaned toward Trent. Amber had talked Joey into coloring with her, and the adults lounged back on their elbows.

"Bet ya Amber falls asleep before the tenth firework goes off," she whispered.

"Deal, because I don't think she'll make five. It's Joey who won't make it to ten."

Melodie smiled, nodding.

It was finally dusk and Joey scampered over to his uncle, claiming his lap for a lounge chair. Not to be outdone, Amber scrambled into Melodie's arms just as the first oohs and ahhs were exclaimed. Melodie watched the sky in wonder, never failing to be amazed at the sights, no matter how many years in a row she'd sat just like this, her neck craned back, her pulse thrumming in anticipation.

Trent won the bet. The fireworks launcher was poised on the far bank of a stretch of the Colorado River that ran through town, yet despite the booming noises, Amber was sound asleep. All it had taken was for her to shut her mouth and her eyes at the same time. Melodie adjusted her position to cradle Amber's head against her shoulder. She knew she could lay her burden on the blanket, but it wasn't often that she was afforded this kind of gift. She couldn't give it up just yet.

In fact, she was drawn away from the magnificent display in the sky to watch the utter, innocent perfection of the face of a sleeping child. Just as they had the night she'd tucked Amber into bed at Trent's, Melodie's eyes filled with tears. Through her watery vision, she looked over at Joey, peacefully asleep on Trent's chest, and then back at Amber.

Did Bridgette have any idea how lucky she was? She had two beautiful, engaging children, and she had a man who was madly in love with her. A person couldn't be in a room with her and Glen for more than a minute and not figure that out. Her life might have started out rough, but there couldn't be a more romantic, fairy-tale ending than the one Bridgette was living.

Melodie wasn't usually the envious type, but at the moment, she would have given almost anything to have what Bridgette had. Unfortunately that *almost* included marriage, and that was where Melodie drew the line. She might be wistful, but she wasn't stupid. She couldn't get the picture out of her mind of her friends giving up their identities one by one after they got married. Even though they seemed happy, Melodie couldn't understand how they could betray themselves that way. If marriage meant always putting her dreams last, just because her husband made more money, then she didn't have what it took to make that kind of commitment.

Heaven knew that she'd bent more than one rule in her life, but her one absolutely inviolate code was that she would never have a child unless she was married. It made for a lovely catch-22. More than one of her friends had pointed out that this was the nineties, after all, and she could have a child on her own if she wanted. But that choice wasn't right for her.

She knew it was illogical, but she couldn't help how she felt. She'd grown up desperately wanting her parents to notice her, and knew the heartache when it hadn't happened. For all that she had a wealth of love to give, she would never make a child start out with a giant hole in his or her life from the get go.

No matter how archaic, she believed with her whole heart that a child should grow up in a home where his or her parents were madly in love and shared that love with the child. A love that allowed both partners space to grow. That allowed for idiosyncrasies and foibles. And no man would ever love her that way. She was asking the impossible to find someone who adored her to distraction but would not smother her.

Trent was the perfect example. He was looking for a female version of himself, the perfect companion for a man on his way up in the business world. Heck, even Glen was expecting Bridgette to follow him as his job commanded. Men never changed.

A cascade of fireworks burst through the sky, breaking her train of thought. She added her "Oooh" to those of the folks around them. The wind blew a strand of hair across her cheek to tickle her nose and the smell of the sunbaked earth still permeated the air.

"That was beautiful," Trent said as the set started to fade.

"Yes, it was."

He must have noticed the distant sound to her voice, for he turned his head to look at her. "I think that last burst especially reminded me of you."

He succeeded in getting her attention. "Really? Why?"

"The concentric circles of clashing colors made me think of your wild outfits."

Melodie gave him a wry grin. "You know, I've only worn tie-dye one time in your presence, but you're never going to let me live it down."

Trent chuckled. "You're probably right. I can even see your wedding announcement. The Sunday paper will read, 'The bride wore a gown of chartreuse and lime green tie-dye. Her attendants wore—'"

"Oh, stop it," she managed to say around a laugh, amused despite her earlier dark thoughts.

The finale drew their eyes back to the sky as the night was filled with rapid-fire volleys of fireworks. Then a relative quiet fell as thousands of people started packing their gear to head home. It always made Melodie a little sad, even though her adult brain knew the magic had to end.

With both kids sacked out, Trent insisted she stay comfortable while he ran the cooler and picnic basket to the car. He returned shortly and carried Joey and the blanket, leaving her only Amber to worry about. Melodie quickly found that for all Amber's slender build, a sleeping child was deadweight. She was grateful when they reached the car and strapped both kids into the back seat.

Because of Trent's strategic planning, they only had a few minutes' wait to get into the flow of traffic. From Town Lake, it wasn't much more than a fifteen-minute drive to her house.

Since he would never be out of sight of the car, Trent could leave the kids sleeping in the back seat while he once again walked her to her porch. She was almost embarrassed at her relief that the children were an ideal excuse to keep the goodbyes short. For just an instant she had images of them as a family, of coming home and carrying the kids inside to tuck into bed. The perfect domestic scene. But she quickly forced the thought away, and nervousness filled the vacant spot.

"I had a nice time," Trent said, his voice matching the quiet night around them.

"Me, too. Thank you for picking me up."

Trent shoved his hands in his pockets and rocked on the sides of his feet. Melodie was surprised. It was the first time she'd seen him nervous.

"Melodie, this probably isn't a good time to bring this up, but then again, I don't know that there ever will be. I called the garage where I had your car towed. Al's a friend of mine, and he says your car's going to cost more than it's worth to fix. He suggests you junk it and get a new one."

Melodie stared at him, assimilating this latest bombshell. Moving backward, she sat on the vinyl-covered cushions on her wicker love seat. She dropped her forehead into her hands. After a moment, her shoulders started shaking.

"Melodie, I'm sorry. I didn't think this would hit you quite this hard."

She couldn't help it. Her shoulders started shaking harder.

"Melodie! I'm really sorry. I knew you'd be calling Al tomorrow and I wanted to break the news before he did. If it would help, I'd be happy to help you look for a new car."

Finally she was able to drag a gasping breath into her lungs, and her silent bellows of laughter finally took voice.

Trent jumped back, looking for all the world as though he thought she'd gone insane, but she couldn't stop laughing long enough to reassure him. How could she explain that hysterical laughter was her only choice besides hysterical tears? After all, in the course of a month, her roommate had left her high and dry, she had rent due on her house and her studio, she was working herself into a coma on a project that could be a boom or a bust and she'd made love to a man who'd stolen her soul.

A dead car? No big deal!

"Melodie?" Trent took her by the shoulders and gave her a little shake. "Melodie, stop it."

She reduced herself to gasping hums with a few giggles now and then until she finally got herself under control.

"Oh, Trent, now I'm sorry. I didn't mean to scare you, but if you only knew...."

"If I only knew what?"

She shook her head, taking a deep breath. "Nothing. I've got a grip now, don't worry."

Trent ran his fingers through his perfectly styled hair. "Jeez, Melodie, please don't do that to me again."

She barely stifled a giggle. "I'll do my best."

"Listen, I need to get the kids home, but tomorrow, after the shoot, I'll run you by my house and you can use my truck until you decide what to do."

"I can't do that—"

"Please, damn it, don't argue with me right now. I've got three vehicles. I can only drive one at a time."

Her internal level of absurdity was so high, she started to tease him about his reluctance to offer her his luxury car, but in the end decided to leave it alone. He'd probably pick her up bodily and take her to the local sanitarium.

"Okay, Trent. We'll talk about it tomorrow."

"I'll pick you up at eight, for the final shoot?"

"Eight it is."

She knew he would not leave until she was inside and heard her locks catch so she dutifully left him standing on the porch.

By the time she got into bed, her desire to laugh had drained away as thoroughly as the water from her shower had swirled and disappeared at her feet. Maybe all that laughter had been the proverbial last straw, leaving her exhausted and broken. Although it would be logical for her thoughts to be centered on her deceased car, she couldn't even dredge up a good dose of worry. It was the least of her problems. She'd been without a car before and survived.

What her mind would not let go of was the picture of Trent, a sleepy child on his lap, tilting his head to look at her with a heart-stopping smile on his face. And fireworks raining down behind his head.

She realized that having a glimpse of the perfect family, something she believed she could never have, was nearly her undoing. Holding the sleeping Amber while Trent had held Joey... The image burned as hotly in her mind as any of those magnificent volleys across the sky, only to fade out just as quickly.

In the end, it didn't matter what she felt for Trent. He could never love someone like her. He was looking for the perfect wife, and not only was she about as far from perfect as someone could get, she was also completely unsuitable as wife material. He needed someone who looked perpetually elegant and who could throw a dinner party on a moment's notice, not an off-beat redhead who considered cheese puffs the gourmet version of cheese curls.

But her logic didn't stop her from aching with the knowledge of what could never be.

Ten

Melodie made it through the final filming by sheer force of will. Since sleeping had been a joke, she'd spent most of the night psyching herself up. She'd gotten up early, and using every makeup trick at her disposal, she was dressed and ready for the camera long before Trent had knocked at her door.

She poured every ounce of energy she had into being vivacious while the camera was rolling. She smiled and she danced and she instructed until she thought her face would fall off. She encouraged and cajoled and teased the kids. She talked with the team and made impromptu changes with seamless accuracy.

And no one seemed to see that she was dying inside.

"Cut!" Ronald yelled for the last time, stepping from behind his camera and onto the stage area. "Melodie, that was terrific! You were wonderful."

She dredged up one last smile and held it as Ronald hugged her and the children surged around her, their enthusiasm barely contained. She even made it through the congratulations of the parents before she finally excused herself and made her way to the ladies' lounge.

It was over, thank God. Now it was up to the editors to splice and paste and add credits and remove flubs and do whatever other magic it was that editors did to make a video polished.

Thankful to be alone, she braced one weary arm on the sink and used her other hand to turn the tap. She splashed her face over and over with cold water, unmindful of the spreading wetness changing her fuchsia stripe to cherry red. It didn't matter anymore.

But the water couldn't wash away the memory of Trent's face as she'd worked. She'd tried not to look at him, but a glance every now and then had been inevitable. And each one had given her a glimpse of a hunger in his eyes that stole a tiny bit more of her reserve.

A tentative knock on the bathroom door broke her trance.

"Melodie? It's Bridgette. Can I come in?"

She wanted to scream at Bridgette to leave her alone. Instead, she closed her eyes against the stab of shame she felt at her churlishness.

"Yes, come in."

The door swung inward and closed slowly behind Bridgette as she took a step inside.

"Are you all right?"

Okay, so maybe someone had noticed. Her short laugh contained no humor. "Yeah, I'm fine."

Needing to escape from the recrimination of her own reflection, and unable to meet Bridgette's eyes, Melodie turned away and sat on the padded bench. She leaned back against the dark paneling and stared unseeing at the print of van Gogh's sunflowers gracing the opposite wall.

"I was coming in to add my congratulations to all of the others," Bridgette started, joining Melodie on the long seat, "but I'm getting the impression you'd rather not hear that again."

Melodie gave her a weak shrug. "Not really."

"What's wrong? Can I help?" Bridgette asked softly, putting a friendly hand on Melodie's weary shoulder.

"No, but thanks for trying. I'm just really tired."

Bridgette stiffened a bit. "It's my brother, isn't it? If that stubborn idiot has hurt you—"

"What are you talking about?" Melodie's confusion was real.

But Bridgette was on a roll. "That pigheaded, obstinate idiot! He's so blinded by his one-track thinking, he can't see what's right in front of his nose. I'm going to—"

"Bridgette! What are you going on about? Trent didn't do anything to me."

Well, that wasn't exactly true, but Melodie had no intention of using Bridgette as a mother-confessor.

Bridgette gave her a long, hard look that brooked no nonsense. "Melodie, I know we've only been friends for a few weeks now, but if you're going to sit there and tell me you don't love my brother as much as he loves you, I'm going to punch something."

Melodie found humor somewhere in all the madness. "You are a truly sweet woman, and I appreciate what you're trying to do, but your brother doesn't love me. And even if he did, we're completely wrong for each other. We would make each other miserable, so please, give up this fantasy that somehow we're going to be a couple. It just isn't going to happen."

Bridgette let the subject drop. "Is Trent taking you home?"

She felt a moment of panic. She had been so single-mindedly focused when he'd picked her up that she'd forgotten about his insistence that she borrow one of his vehicles.

That would mean he would be taking her to his house. Even if the trip was just to pick up his truck, she didn't think she could handle being so near the place where she'd given her soul away for the first and last time. But she didn't have any choice. For once, she admitted she didn't have the energy to be a super-woman. If she could get through the next few days, she'd go by the bank and wipe out her savings to buy some type of functional car. But for right now, it was all she could do to get from minute to minute.

Soon the headache that was building at the back of her head would come on full force. Then she would be lucky to stay upright. She had to make a decision. And fast.

"He said he'd do it, but would you mind taking me instead? I hate to sound like a child, but I just can't take any more."

"That's not childish, Melodie, just human." Bridgette pulled her in for a hug. "Of course I'll take you home."

The two women walked together across the long studio and joined the remaining stragglers leaving the building.

Trent moved beside her. "Are you ready to go?"

Calling on the last of her courage, she met his eyes. "Trent, I apologize for the sudden change in plans, but Bridgette's going to give me a ride. I'll call you later about the truck."

She felt him withdraw even though he didn't move an inch. She honestly hadn't intended to insult him, but maybe the gods would forgive her lack of manners just this once. And maybe she could finagle a two-for-one deal and receive absolution for her bald-faced lie about calling him at the same time....

"Miss Melodie, are you okay?"

Amber had glided forward and put her little hand in Melodie's. She looked up with distress etched on her little face.

Joey moved closer, as well, and Melodie was touched by his obvious concern.

"Yeah," he announced after studying her face, "you don't look so hot."

"Joey!" Bridgette exclaimed, her face flushing that particular shade of mother's mortification.

Melodie had to laugh. "It's all right, Bridgette." She looked down at the kids. "I'm fine, guys. Thanks for asking. But I think we need to clear out of here so the next group of people can get to work."

Reassured, the children led the way outside, and Melodie managed to get into Bridgette's car without further stalling.

She knew, though, as they pulled away and she caught a glimpse of Trent standing by his car, that she might have gotten away this time, but she was far from her last confrontation with him.

* * *

Trent wielded the hedge trimmer with vicious strokes, but found his feeling of rejection was not ebbing with each chop as he'd hoped. Hard, physical exercise had seemed the best strategy an hour ago. Now he was tired and frustrated instead of energized and frustrated.

Wiping sweat from his forehead with the back of his hand, he retreated to the stone bench under the towering live oak that shaded a good third of his backyard. Spearing the tips of the trimmer into the soft grass, he absentmindedly dug a hole as his thoughts wandered.

What was wrong with him, he decided, was that he had been allowing himself to get off track. He's been so hyperfocused before he'd met Melodie that she'd caught him by surprise. She hadn't been what he'd thought he was looking for, so she'd slipped past his guard while he was distracted.

The thing to do was get his head back in order and forget this infatuation that had blindsided him. That was it! It was just an infatuation, and if he would return to his former discipline, he'd have his system free of her in no time.

He almost had himself convinced to go inside, take a shower and find Erin's phone number. He'd give her a call and, surely, spending the evening with someone who was more his type would take care of this once and for all.

Then Bridgette came storming around the corner of the house and his little bubble of inspiration burst.

"You are the stupidest, most stubborn, irritating lump of a horse's behind I have ever had the privilege to set my eyes on. I can't believe you are so blind. . . ."

Trent wasn't sure exactly what he'd done to earn her ire, but he made no attempt to stop her tirade. When Bridgette was on a roll, it was best to let her burn herself out. Besides, he wasn't in the mood to pacify his sister, even if she did mean the world to him. He had troubles of his own he hadn't found a way to deal with, namely one beautiful woman with long red hair who had branded him with her smile and a touch.

"...you listening to me? Trenton, I'm talking to you!"

"No, sweetie, you're haranguing me. There's a difference."

"Don't you patronize me, Trenton James Laroquette. And don't think for one minute I didn't see that deer-in-the-headlights look that came over you. Well, you'd just better prick those ears, boy, 'cause I'm not done—"

"Where are the kids?"

"They're inside watching a video. And you'd better believe that you're gonna pay attention, too—"

"All right, but would you like to sit down for the reading of the riot act?"

Bridgette stomped her petite foot. "No, I don't want to sit down! I harangue much better standing up, thank you."

"Sis, I wouldn't dream of denying the heinous crimes I'm so obviously guilty of, but would you mind informing me of just a couple of the particulars?"

She scoffed at him. A truly bad sign.

"As if you didn't know. I don't know how you can stand yourself after what you've done. Melodie is one of the sweetest people I have ever met—"

"Melodie? What about her? Is something wrong?"

"Well, of course something's wrong, as if you didn't know. But then again, you're a man, aren't you? How silly of me to think you'd notice—"

"Bridgette."

The clear warning in his voice stopped her.

Her voice dropped several notches. "Just what did you do to her anyway? She got through the video on sheer guts. When I went into the ladies' lounge with her, it was like seeing a brilliant flashlight with the batteries suddenly drained dry."

Trent felt his gut clench with guilt, but on the heels of that reaction came defensiveness. "Who says I did anything to her?"

Bridgette's face lost its animation and became coldly earnest. "Don't you do it, too. Melodie tried to make me believe that there's nothing between you, but I've watched electricity arc between the two of you every time you're in the same room. Why are you both being so stubborn?"

Trent plunged the shears into the ground with a telling thrust and left them. He ran his hands over his face in a weary gesture.

"She and I came together and it was like spontaneous combustion. But ever since, she's treated me like I've got the plague. I don't know what I did to make her act this way."

"Maybe she's scared. Or maybe you told her that nonsense about how you're bride hunting and it hurt her pride."

Trent's gaze jerked to hers. "Well, I've got pride, too. A man doesn't like being rejected out of hand any more than a woman does. Besides, *you're* the one who filled her ears about my future plans. Which you have all wrong, by the way."

"Yeah, right. You practically have an application form for your candidates to fill out in triplicate."

Trent wouldn't have expected her gibe to sting as much as it did. He thought he'd hidden it until Bridgette hurried over to sit beside him. She put her head on his shoulder, unmindful of his shirt being damp with sweat.

"I'm sorry, Trent. I didn't mean to hurt your feelings."

"It's okay—"

"No, it's not. I get all riled up and I say things I shouldn't.... I always have. You know that. I just love you so much, and I want you to be happy. Melodie is perfect for you, I just know it. And I don't have time to help you get this straightened out before—"

Her abrupt pause ignited his curiosity. "What do you mean you don't have time? Not that I'm inviting your butting in, mind you." He looked at her sharply. "Before what?"

Bridgette twisted her hands together. "I've been putting off telling you this because we've had so much going on and I was so hoping things would get going between you and Melodie, and the kids have kept me so busy and—"

"Whoa! Take a breath every fifteenth word or so, sis! Just spit it out."

"Glen and I are moving to Chicago at the end of next month. He's taken a job with that big cable company he told you about."

Trent felt vaguely out of breath. He'd never expected his sister to plan her life around him, but the thought of her being so far away stunned him. She and the kids had been such an important part of his life for so long now.

He caught himself before his thoughts ran too far away and found a smile somewhere deep inside him. "Hey, congratulations, sweetie." He hugged Bridgette to him and kissed her forehead. "Is the wedding going to be here or in Chicago?"

Bridgette laughed. "You pretend to be such a man of the nineties, but you really mean the 1890s. Who says we're getting married?"

Trent knew a moment of real fear before he realized his sister had yanked his chain but good. "Very funny."

She started giggling and danced away, getting a running start before he started chasing her. He caught her near the pool, swinging her into his arms. He held her over the deep end as she gasped and begged for mercy.

"I'm sorry, Trent. I just couldn't resist teasing you. Please don't throw me in!"

He let her down and hugged her close. "I'm happy for you, brat. Really I am."

She hugged him fiercely in return. "Thank you. We're having the wedding in Chicago after we get settled. You know most of Glen's folks are in Milwaukee, so it's a lot closer for them. You're all I have, so I thought you might not mind coming up there."

"You know nothing could keep me away."

She pulled out of his embrace and walked toward the house with his arm draped over her shoulders and hers wrapped around his waist. "So now we've finished with me. What about you and Melodie?"

"I don't have an answer for you, sis."

"Well, you're not going to give up without a fight, are you? That's not the Trenton Laroquette I know."

He acknowledged her attempt but shook his head. "This is different somehow. I plan on trying to see her again, but I'm not hopeful that she'll want to see me."

"So go take a shower and give it a try. There's no time like the present."

Trent rolled his eyes. "Platitudes, just what I need."

But he did as she suggested. As he showered, he found that all he could think about was getting to Melodie's and telling her about Bridgette and the kids. Somehow he knew that she was the only one who could understand what this was going to mean to him. And he needed to be with her because—

He went still and a smile spread over his face.

Because he was in love with her. All logic to the contrary, he was head over heels in love with a leggy redhead who would probably drive him to distraction. She was nothing like the women he'd thought would be perfect for him. There was a saying in the legal community that a man who would defend himself has a fool for a client. Well, maybe a man who tried to pick a mate by logic was just as big a fool.

If his candidate list had been on paper, he would have made the symbolic gesture of tearing it up. Since it was all in his head, he pressed a mental delete key and let the questionnaire fade from his memory. He'd found the perfect woman and she would never have passed his silly test. And thank heaven for that! Instead of finding what he was asking for, he had found much more than he deserved.

He wanted so much more now, more than a hostess or a mere companion. If he wanted a hostess, he could hire one, and he wanted a friend, a lover, a match to the other half of his soul.

And now that he'd found her, he could only pray that he could make her want the same things from him, since all the evidence indicated that Melodie did not feel similarly inclined. She gave every appearance of wanting nothing to do with him. He could only hope the evidence was misleading.

Using the excuse of returning the forgotten plate she'd used for her lemon bars last night, Trent headed out in the bright sunlight toward Melodie's house.

When the doorbell rang, Melodie found her back hurting from several non-stop hours of channel surfing. Dressed in a purple tie-dyed shirt and white shorts, she was hardly in the mood for company. Hopefully it would be the neighborhood kids selling yet another round of candy bars. She needed a chocolate fix. After all, wasn't that the most renowned cure for depression? If so, maybe she'd better buy a whole case.

"Hel—"

Trent, freshly showered and shaved and wearing pleated slacks and a sports shirt, didn't look like any student she'd ever gone to school with.

"—lo, Trent. I...um...didn't expect to see you here."

"I'm sorry I didn't call first. I know I should have."

She felt her face heat and she plucked at her shirt. "You could at least have given me a chance to change."

She shouldn't want to change, she reminded herself. She shouldn't be wishing she'd had fair warning so she could have put on that brand-new shorts set she'd bought and thrown some makeup on her face, which she knew looked pale and strained. She shouldn't be regretting that she'd used unscented lotion on her legs after her shower instead of the fragrant body cream Serena had given her for Christmas. And she shouldn't be so torn between her breathless delight at seeing him and her agonizing wish that he would go away.

He smiled. "Hey, at least they're not piggy leggings. Although—" he tilted his head slightly to the right "—to tell you the truth, I kinda liked the little guys on you."

How could she have forgotten, in the mere hours since she'd left the studio, how dark his hair was and how blue it made his eyes appear? How could seeing him now pack just as much punch as the first time she'd set eyes on him?

The intensity of his appraisal made her pulse skyrocket. Maybe near exhaustion and a refreshing nap made for clarity of thought, although she doubted it. Whatever the reason, the truth would no longer be denied. With one look at his face, so tentative, so hesitant, she had to finally admit she was in love with him. Not that it made any difference in the grand scheme of things, of course, but she couldn't pretend any longer that her heart had any intention of listening to her head. All her logical, rational arguments for why she couldn't possibly be feeling this way had the longevity of a burst from a Roman candle.

"Um, thanks." She realized belatedly that she was hanging on to the door for dear life. "Would you like to come in? I was just doing a little channel surfing to unwind." *And trying to get you out of my mind, out of my heart, out of my soul.*

"Sure. Oh, here." He handed her the plate he'd tucked under his arm.

"I wasn't exactly in a rush for it, but you're sweet to bring it over."

She watched, amazed, as a slight flush stained his cheeks.

"Well, to be honest, I kinda used it as an excuse. With the way you left the studio earlier, I wasn't sure you'd want to see me."

She couldn't tell him that she wanted to see him more than anything she'd ever wanted, especially since she hadn't had time to deal with her new revelations about her feelings. She thought she'd known what it was to be vulnerable. Now she nearly laughed to realize how naive she'd been. She hadn't had a clue.

They each took one end of her couch, and Melodie twisted sideways, one leg tucked comfortably underneath her. "Since you're being honest, I will be, too. When I left the studio, I was completely drained. I'd given everything I had to finish the video—"

"You were great, by the way."

"I appreciate that, but I needed to get home and crash. I took a shower before grabbing a nap, so I'm feeling better."

"I'm glad. You kinda scared me."

"I didn't mean to." But how could she have faced him, as fragile as she'd been? He had no idea what power his mere presence had on her. And she had to be careful that he never found out.

"Please don't apologize. I'm just glad you're all right."

Their pleasant exchanges ground to a halt. Obviously Trent was as uncertain as she was. And she wasn't sure what to do. She was still feeling exposed, nervous, and he was much too close.

She cleared her throat. "So, has Amber come down off cloud nine yet?"

Something passed across Trent's face, filling his eyes with sorrow. He masked it quickly, but she was sure she'd glimpsed something deep. She couldn't imagine what could have happened to make him work so hard to pretend nothing was wrong.

"Trent? What's the matter?"

He smiled oddly, as though the gesture was hard won.

"Bridgette told me this afternoon that she and Glen are moving to Chicago. Glen got a job offer he's been waiting for."

Melodie felt a stab of sadness that was out of proportion to the announcement. Yes, she'd grown fond of Bridgette and the kids in a very short time, but she shouldn't feel devastated to hear they were moving.

And if she felt this way, what must Trent be feeling?

"Trent, I'm sorry."

She couldn't stop herself. She wasn't sure she even wanted to. But of her own volition she moved closer and let him pull her into his arms for an embrace that nearly crushed her ribs. He buried his mouth against her neck and held her, breathing deeply.

"I'm feeling selfish, is all. There's nothing I want more than for my sister to be happy. I just wish she could be happy here in Austin."

Trent released her and they shifted comfortably on the couch, much closer now but not touching. She saw the love he had for Bridgette and felt a moment of envy that made her ashamed. In his own way, Nathan had loved her, but she and her brother had had nothing like the bond Trent and Bridgette shared.

As if he'd read her thoughts, Trent continued. "I suppose I shouldn't complain. She'll only be a plane ticket away."

He looked at her, and she knew he saw the empathy lurking behind her eyes.

"You're very lucky, Trent."

He nodded. "I know." He leaned forward and took her hand. "Hey, I didn't mean to make you sad, too."

Her smile was as weak as his had been. "I can't explain it. I haven't known Bridgette and the kids for very long, and yet I feel like crying all of a sudden. I'm going to miss them."

"You know, I'd have to say almost the same thing," Trent said, looking down at his hands. "I think I told you that we didn't grow up together, and in fact, they didn't come into my life in a real way until a few years ago."

He took a deep breath and held it for a long moment. When he sighed, she felt her heart twist. She could barely hear his next words.

"I don't know what I'll do without them."

In a moment of perfect clarity, Melodie realized what it was about Trent that frightened her so. She'd been using the excuse that he was looking for a wife as an excuse to stay distant. Then she'd told herself she wasn't his type. But now she knew. Now she understood.

Trent was the kind of man who felt. Deeply. He didn't hide from his emotions like every other man she'd chosen. Oh, he was hardly the new in-touch-with-his-feminine-side kind of guy, although she wouldn't fall over in a faint if he did cry. But she suddenly was sure that Trent gave of himself from the bottom of his soul. She'd been right when she'd mentally accused him of looking at marriage as he did his job. But she hadn't understood her own assumption. He *would* treat his marriage like his job, in the respect that he would pour himself into it, heart, body and soul, and he would be the kind of husband most women could only dream about.

And just as she'd known the first time, she knew she and Trent were going to end up making love sometime tonight. She'd been avoiding him because she knew her attraction to him was undeniable, a force that would not be dissuaded. She'd known that if an opportunity arose to be with him, as they were now—talking quietly, intimately—that the evening's end was as predictable as sunrise. And just like the last time, she wasn't going to pretend it wasn't happening.

But this time she would approach the experience differently. The last time, she hadn't known she was in love with him. Now she knew. She could take this moment and cherish it, store it to remember in the years to come as one of the most special events in her life. Maybe it would be enough to sustain her when he went away and got on with his life.

She hadn't realized how lost in her own thoughts she had been until her hearing popped back in as though her ear had just depressurized.

"...but she is finally happy and at peace. I used to wonder if that would ever happen."

Melodie was fairly confident he was talking about Bridgette so she picked up the conversation. "I know she's had it pretty rough. She deserves this."

Trent nodded. "Yes, she does."

His face flushed and took on a delightfully bashful expression.

"Forgive me. I didn't mean to run off at the mouth like that."

"Please don't apologize." Melodie easily absolved him, since she'd been lost in her own thoughts. "I'm just glad you felt you could talk to me."

He held her eyes for a long moment. "I am, too. I wish we hadn't been so distant since Saturday."

It was her turn to flush. "You're being too kind. You know I was avoiding you."

The corner of his mouth twitched. "Yes, and I couldn't figure out what I did wrong."

"Did you ever stop to think you didn't do anything wrong? That it might not be you at all?"

"Actually, yes, but I still had a hard time with it."

He stopped her before she could respond. "And don't apologize. I'm just glad you're not avoiding me anymore."

With deliberate slowness, Melodie leaned forward and pressed her mouth to his, a whisper-soft kiss that said, "I'm glad you're here."

When she leaned away to look into his eyes, he smiled, a gentle curving of his full, soft lips that answered, "So am I."

Eleven

Trent reached up and unclasped the barrette that held her hair away from her face.

"I love doing this," he said as he ran his fingers through the long tresses and fanned them over her shoulders in a rain of russet silk. "Pulling pins from your hair is almost as exciting as undressing you."

His lips quirked as he took his eyes from her hair and returned to her face. "Please note I said *almost*."

She smiled softly, trailing kisses along his chin and neck. What was it about this man that his merest touch sent her pulse racing? Her body tingled, anticipating him, yet she wanted this moment to go on forever as his mouth and his hands explored the contours of her body.

Her breath caught when his fingers slipped under the hem of her T-shirt to trace the swell of her breast.

It wasn't as if he hadn't done this before, but somehow, with Trent, everything felt new, bringing up a longing in her she had thought deeply buried. The longing to be unique, special, important. Trent made her feel those things.

And it scared her.

That was why she'd run away the first time. That was what she'd forgotten until this moment when the feelings rushed over her, awakening again the slumbering beasts of her innermost fear and insecurity.

It took her a moment to realize she had gone still. Trent sat watching her with worry etched on his brow.

"Trent, I—"

When the telephone rang, they both froze. With a wry grimace, she picked up the phone.

"Mother?" She answered the voice, wriggling out of his arms to sit beside him on the couch. "Well, actually, I have company. What did you need?"

He tried to stand, intending to move away and give her some privacy, but she caught his arm and sent him a look that clearly said, "Please stay." He needed no further urging to settle down again and placed a hand on her knee.

"In the hospital? When? Is he all right?"

The play of emotions across her face tugged at him. In flashes, he'd seen surprise, concern and now anger.

"Dad's been in the hospital for three days and you're just now calling me?" Her fingers clasped his almost painfully as she listened.

"I know you hate the answering machine, Mother, but don't you think this once you could have forced yourself?"

Color drained from her face only to rush back in a vivid blush. "Mother, I'm not going to apologize for not staying home in case you *might* call. I have a job and a social life."

Melodie's back stiffened and he could feel her defensiveness.

"I'm sorry, Mother, but I can't—"

Trent couldn't make out the words, but heard a decidedly scolding tone from the receiver, as if Melodie's mother had raised her voice.

"Mother, listen to me. I would take you to the cemetery and then to the hospital, but I don't have a car—"

Trent got her attention and mouthed, "I'll take you." She shook her head, but he nodded "yes" just as emphatically. She covered the mouthpiece and whispered, "She lives in Buda. That's too far away."

"No it's not," he whispered back. "Melodie, please let me help."

With a resigned sigh, she removed her hand from the speaker. "Wait, Mother. I have a friend who doesn't mind—"

Melodie closed her eyes. "Mother, could you just stop a minute? It's not that I don't want to take you...no...Mother...*Mother!*"

She took a deep breath. "If you want to wait for Aunt Janie, then go ahead. I'm telling you that a friend has offered to help, and we'll come out and get you right now. It's up to you."

Eventually Melodie hung up the phone.

"Melodie, is your father all right?"

Trent's soft inquiry brought her out of her thoughts. "He's been in the hospital having some tests run on his heart. Mother says he passed out the other day and it scared the daylights out of her.''

''I would imagine so.''

''He's at South Austin Medical Center, but we have to go into Buda to get Mother.''

''That's not a problem.''

''I really appreciate this. . . .''

He turned her by her shoulders and urged her down the hall. ''Get your shoes and we'll get going.''

She felt wrung-out. Her mother was the one person on Earth who could do that to her in less than three minutes. She wondered why, with all the billions of dollars spent on medical research, a cure couldn't be found for motheritis.

She hurriedly put on a bra and a cotton camp shirt, tucking it into her shorts without thinking. Women may have burned their bras and walk unrestricted in New York City, but they didn't on the streets of Buda, Texas.

With deft movements, she braided her hair and let it hang down her back. After slipping on a pair of sandals, she was ready.

Trent was reviewing her eclectic collection of CDs as he waited. He turned when he heard her and looked her over with an appreciative eye. She fought against an urge to explain.

''Are you sure you want to do this?'' she asked as she found her keys and her purse.

''It's a little late to ask now, don't you think?''

She followed him out the door and turned to lock it. ''Probably, but I think the rules say you have to ask at least one rhetorical question in every awkward situation.''

''Good, then we've taken care of that one, at least.''

She buckled her seat belt as Trent settled into the driver's side. He wouldn't need instructions until they got into Buda proper. She hardly needed to give him directions to the Interstate.

With the late-afternoon sun glaring into her window, Melodie shifted just enough to cast a glance at Trent that contained at least some of her returning good-nature.

"I should probably warn you about my mother. And my father for that matter."

"You don't have to."

"Yes, I do. You have no idea—"

"Melodie, I'm not doing this for your mother. I'm doing it for you. It doesn't matter what your parents think of me as long as it doesn't matter to you."

Melodie sat back in semishock to realize it wasn't what her parents thought of him that had her preoccupied, it was what he would think of her parents. She shouldn't care what he thought, but she'd be lying if she said she didn't. Trent was so suave, so sophisticated, so upper-class; she was ashamed to admit she was embarrassed for him to see the house she grew up in. Oh, it was neat and clean and tidy, but the furniture was twenty years old and hardly carried sophisticated labels.

She guessed she was something of a snob, if she had to confess. She pretended to be such a free-thinking woman, yet she didn't want Trent to know her mother had been a hairdresser and her father a small-time farmer. If her grandfather hadn't managed to leave her dad a small inheritance to bolster their Social Security, she would probably be supporting them.

Now that was a scary thought.

"This may seem like an obvious question, but I take it your mother doesn't drive?"

Once again, Trent pulled her from her reverie. "Well, if you consider the streets of Buda 'driving,' I can say yes, but Mother has never, ever driven on the highway or in Austin, which is probably a good thing. She's seventy-two, so now's no time for her to start. Dad's seventy-five and still drives well, though. Her sister, my aunt Janie, lives in Buda, too, and takes Mother around if Dad can't."

Miles passed without her being aware, and all too soon they were exiting the highway. She directed him through the streets to her parents' small acreage.

"Buda wasn't always this thriving metropolis," she joked as they passed through "downtown." Some of the shops hadn't changed in twenty years. Or more.

"The boom is fairly recent," he agreed, turning left onto the dirt road that led back to the house. "I understand there are the real Buda residents, and then there are the people who've moved here to escape Austin taxes."

Melodie raised an eyebrow in surprise. "You know more about Buda than I would have thought."

He smiled at her. "I've lived in Austin all my life, Melodie. Buda isn't Shangri-la, hidden in the mists from prying eyes."

"That's for sure," she muttered, opening her door as they pulled to a stop.

She led the way up the steps to a small house. Trent noted absently that the yard was well kept, the flowers lining the walk a little weary from the incessant summer sun but otherwise bright and weed-free. The porch was neatly swept and the swing looked well used, as did the wooden rockers. Melodie opened the screen and knocked twice before opening the door.

"Mother, we're here," she called loudly, looking over her shoulder and motioning him in with a wave.

The front door led directly into the living room. They passed behind the couch and on back to the combined kitchen/dining room. A hallway branched off to the right, and he assumed there would be three bedrooms and a bath as equally neat and tidy.

The kitchen was empty, as Melodie had expected. They returned to the living room, and Melodie directed him to the couch and went down the hallway to search for her mother.

Trenton had plenty of time to browse. On the long wall was a series of pictures of Melodie and her brother, from infancy through the gap-toothed school years and on to graduation.

Pictures of Melodie were included on the wall, but the room was a shrine to her brother. An eleven-by-fourteen of him in his Marine uniform took center stage. Black fabric was draped around the edges of the frame. On the television, another picture of him in uniform stood sentinel, with a case display of his medals standing upright on the side. A flag, folded in the traditional triangle, sat in an oak-and-glass frame on a small table beside the console. Next to the frame lay an arrangement of plastic flowers bound together.

He took another glance around the room. There were no pictures of Melodie taken since her high school graduation.

Female voices made him turn. He put on his most professional smile, stepping forward with his hand out.

"Mrs. Allford? I'm Trenton Laroquette. It's nice to meet you."

Trenton wasn't sure exactly what he'd been anticipating, but Mrs. Allford surprised him. She was slender, like Melodie, but much shorter. Her hair was pure silver, pulled back from her face in a bun. Somehow he'd been ready for old lady blue. And while her pantsuit was polyester, it was cut in a relatively current style that flattered her. Her pearls seemed real, and her white handbag was patent leather.

"It's nice to meet you, Mr. Laroquette," Mrs. Allford said, shaking his hand and releasing it. "I see you were looking at the pictures of our boy. We lost Nathan six years ago—I guess you've heard."

Trenton glanced at Melodie before looking back at her mother. "Melodie mentioned it, yes. Please accept my condolences."

"It was such a tragedy." Mrs. Allford moved across the room in brisk little steps and gave the picture on the wall an infinitesimal nudge. "Well," she said, hitching her purse to the crook of her arm and picking up the flowers. "We'd best be going."

Like a general leading her troops, she led the way outside, then let them pass through before locking the door. She walked toward Trenton's car as though he'd driven her thousands of places before.

Melodie's face might have seemed emotionless to someone who didn't know her, but Trenton saw the tightness in her jaw, the way she was forcing her hands to stay relaxed. He wanted to grab her, hold her close and ease her anxiety, but he doubted she would appreciate the gesture at this moment.

Trenton moved and opened the door for Mrs. Allford, closing it when she had settled herself in the front seat. He held the driver door for Melodie and moved his seat forward for her to fold herself into the back. The arrangement felt awkward, but he didn't know what else to do.

He headed out of town at her direction.

"I'm sure Melodie doesn't remember," Mrs. Allford informed him, straightening the sleeve of her jacket, "but this is the anniversary of the day we heard the news about our Nathan. I always ask her to join me when I take flowers to his grave, but she's always too busy."

"Mother, I'm sure Trent would rather not hear a litany of my shortcomings."

Trent heard Melodie speaking through nearly clenched teeth. His hands tightened on the steering wheel. Maybe one advantage of not having a mother was missing this kind of tension.

Thankfully it didn't take long to reach the small cemetery, which looked exactly as he had expected. Some of the headstones probably dated back to the turn of the century. He followed at a discreet distance while Mrs. Allford went over to the Allford headstone and placed the flowers in the holder built into the monument. Melodie moved to his side and waited with him.

With graveyard vandalism prevalent everywhere, he was surprised the marker was undamaged. As if she'd read his mind, Melodie leaned closer.

"Mother and Dad replace that stupid flower holder at least every year or so. You'd think they'd give up."

Mrs. Allford was saying something in a voice too low to carry. She stood there a moment, patted the headstone and returned to the car. Trenton and Melodie dutifully followed.

The trip to South Austin Medical Center and the visit to Mr. Allford were uneventful. Trenton found the gentleman quiet and polite, if a little irritable from being confined. The man had a permanent farmer's tan, revealed by the unbecoming hospital gown. He was pleasant enough, and although curiosity was in his eyes, he didn't ask any personal questions. Mrs. Allford definitely had the dominant personality.

What struck Trent most of all was that with each passing moment, Melodie became more and more invisible. Her parents both spoke to her, but with no more intimacy than they did to him. When they left the hospital, and when they returned Mrs. Allford to her home, neither parent kissed her nor said more than a pleasant good-night.

It made Trenton indescribably sad.

It was fully dark by the time they reached Melodie's house. Her stomach was in knots and her head ached unbearably. Her worst nightmare had happened, so there was nothing to do now but tell Trent goodbye. He had concrete confirmation that she was unlovable, so he would go away.

She folded her arms around herself and stood awkwardly in the doorway. "Thank you for all the trouble you've gone through for me. I know it was a bother."

"No, actually, it wasn't." He waited for a long moment. "Aren't you going to invite me in?"

She turned reluctantly, her movements wooden as she preceded Trenton in. "Can I get you something to drink?" she asked as she took a glass for herself out of the cabinet. "I'm going to have some iced tea."

"That would be fine."

She was well aware that he watched her every move. She wasn't especially thirsty, but she needed to do something to occupy her hands or she'd scream.

She nearly jumped out of her skin when Trent put his hands on her shoulders and turned her to face him.

"Melodie, it's all right. It's just me."

She almost laughed. *Just* him. Just the man who had stolen her heart and would now walk away to find the perfect bride to go along with his perfect life. Just the man who had made her remember all the dreams she'd hidden away.

She shrugged out of his grasp and handed him his tea. She led the way into the living room and took the only armchair, leaving him the couch.

"Do you want to talk about it?"

She thought that was a woman's line. Weren't men supposed to be insensitive and shy away from a woman in turmoil?

"What would you like to know?"

"Well, could you tell me how you and your parents have become so polarized?"

"What makes you think we haven't always been . . . polarized?"

"I don't know. Have you been?"

"Yes." She took a sip of tea and cleared her throat. "God's not supposed to be able to make mistakes, but I sure can't explain any other reason for why I'm their child. I've never done anything right in my entire life, as far as my mother is concerned."

"You're a marvelously talented, energetic, intelligent, successful businesswoman. You're beautiful and kind. Am I missing something?"

Melodie raised one brow. "I was the child who got sent to the principal for putting glue on the teacher's chair. I got sent home in junior high for my dresses being too short. In high school, I nearly got suspended from the drill team when I was caught in a clinch with my boyfriend in the theater arts center." She met his eyes. "Those are just a few of my minor infractions."

"They're just normal childhood stunts, I'd say."

"You would be able to say that if I were a boy. But this was sixteen years ago in what was then a small, rural town. I was a girl, and I was not doing the ladylike things I should have been doing before getting married and having children."

"I realize your parents are... country folk, but I don't—"

"What it boils down to is that first of all, I'm a mistake. Mother was thirty-five when she had Nathan and almost forty when she had me. She didn't think she was going to have any children, so when she had Nathan, despite the fact that the pregnancy was horrible, she was ecstatic. She was decidedly less thrilled to find out she was going to have to go through that again."

Melodie studied her fingernails while she tried to get her voice under control.

"To add insult to injury," she continued, "I was just too headstrong and rebellious. I've known all my life that their lives would have been much happier if I hadn't shown up. And they'd give their eye teeth for it to be me in that grave and not Nathan."

"Melodie! I didn't see anything to indicate that."

"No, you wouldn't. They hardly announce it over loudspeakers. But I know it."

"Do you think—"

"Trenton, I appreciate what you're trying to do, but my relationship with my parents is pretty much fixed. I don't do anything the way they want me to, and I probably never will. My mother's blood pressure climbs to the ceiling whenever she's around me for long, and my dad just looks at me kind of bewilderedly."

"But you love them. . . ."

"Of course I love them. They're my parents. That doesn't mean we can get along."

Trent put his tea down, stood, and walked over to stand in front of her. He held out his hands, palms up, toward her.

She looked at him, puzzled.

"Come here."

"Trent—"

"Just shut up and come here."

She put her hands in his and let him lift her to her feet. She moved into his arms stiffly, fighting the overwhelming urge to wrap herself around him and never let go.

His arms embraced her, sliding down her back in a soothing, gentle caress. His hands kneaded her taut muscles, and his cheek rubbed the top of her head. She had no idea how long he held her there, but finally the tension drained from her body.

"I'm going to make a giant leap here, Melodie."

She arched her neck to look at him.

He continued. "Just because you don't think your parents love you does not make you unlovable. I think you and your parents are locked into some behaviors that leave a gap you can't bridge. But I do think they love you. You just can't show each other."

"Well, thank you, Dr. Freud."

"I don't know if it's Freudian or not. I didn't major in psychology. I just see someone I... care very much about all tied up in knots. And I want to help."

Melodie extricated herself from his arms and busied herself by picking up their glasses and walking with them to the kitchen. She used the precious seconds to gather her courage and turn back to him.

"Trent, thank you for caring." She forced herself to meet his eyes. In her heart of hearts she knew that when he left tonight she'd never see him again. But she was just too raw and vulnerable to let him go yet. She might pay double for it later, but she wanted one last time with him.

She moved back into his arms and snuggled into his shoulder.

"Melodie—"

"Please," she begged, "don't talk. Just hold me."

He did as she asked. He responded when she lifted her mouth for a kiss. He answered when she demanded more.

She was stunned—and hurt—when he pushed her away a few moments later.

"What did I do wrong?" she managed to ask in a strangled voice. "Don't you want me?"

He traced his finger down her cheek as his eyes burned into hers. "More than anything in the world. But I want you to want *me*, Melodie. Not just a body to make you forget your pain."

"But I do—"

He put a gentle finger on her lips.

"I want to be your lover, Melodie. And much more. But you're not ready. When you are, I'll be here."

She was rooted to the spot as he kissed her forehead, turned and left. When she could move, she picked up a pillow and hurled it at the door.

How dare he! How dare he psychoanalyze her, get her all revved up and then leave!

And what did he mean she wasn't ready? she asked herself as she stormed down the hall to her bedroom, yanking her shirt off as she went.

Her anger built as she jerked on pajamas and slammed herself down on the bed.

How dare he be so... so...

Right.

She punched her pillow with a balled fist. All right, so she wanted to forget the hurt for a few minutes, but that wasn't all she wanted him for. She was in love with him, even though she couldn't let him know that. Just as much as she wanted comforting, she wanted to spend every second she could with him while she had the chance. Before it was too late.

She sat up, clutching her pillow to her stomach.

What did he mean by *"I want to be your lover, Melodie. And much more..."*?

And much more...

She viciously shut down that train of thought. He could have meant a hundred things by that. The last thing she needed to do was to get her hopes up only to have them crushed.

But maybe he had been right about one thing. She and her parents—especially her mother—were locked into their roles. One thing was for certain, nothing was going to change until one of them made a move.

Maybe she was just tired, but she didn't fight the little voice inside her that told her to pick up the phone. Maybe nothing would come out of this, but she'd give it a try.

She dialed the number.

"Mother? This is Melodie...no, nothing's wrong...I just thought I'd check on you... no...no...Mother, please, just listen for a second. All I wanted to do was call you and say...and just tell you...I...I love you, Mother. And I was wondering if we could maybe have lunch or something...what?...yeah, next weekend would be great...."

Twelve

Melodie stood at Trent's door, trying to stop her knees from shaking. The sun was almost down, and the gate had been open so she guessed he was home from the office. If he wasn't, she'd wait until he was. It had been a week since she'd seen him, and she wasn't going to leave until she did. She could have called him, she supposed, but the fact was, she was too chicken. She'd saved up all her courage and she had one shot. She couldn't waste it on the telephone.

She heard the doorknob turn and she called on all her bravado.

"Melodie!"

"Listen, buddy." She took the offensive, moving forward to stab him in the chest with her forefinger. He retreated as she advanced, so she kicked the door shut with her heel. "You left me high and dry last week, and I'm here to collect."

She almost smiled as his expression went from surprise, to confusion, to understanding—and back to surprise. Then it became a wicked grin that he quickly tried to hide.

"Oh, yeah?"

"Yeah. Because of you I've been out to see my mother twice and had a long talk with my dad in the hospital. It's been one heck of a week."

His control on his grin slipped just a little. "Oh, yeah?"

"Yeah. This is all your fault. Now you're going to pay up."

She stopped in her tracks, her bravado failing as she looked around. "You don't have the kids tonight, do you?"

His mouth twitched suspiciously. "No, they're with their mother, as they usually are. My having them so much was due to the project and all the late hours Bridgette was pulling at school."

"Oh." With a deep breath she pulled her mantle back around her. "Darn good thing, too," she spit out, advancing again with serious intent, pulling her ponytail holder off her braid and shaking out her hair.

She didn't fail to see that he was backing carefully down the hall toward his bedroom. She pretended not to notice.

"I suppose I'm in big trouble," he wondered aloud, unbuttoning the cuffs on his shirt.

"The biggest," she assured him, unhitching her belt and pulling it from the loops on her jeans. "You don't leave a lady like that, mister. It's bad form."

"I suppose I'd better make it up to you, then," he decided, slipping out of his shoes and continuing his strategic withdrawal.

Her shoes were a step apart from his. "And if you don't, you'll try again and again and again until you get it right."

"Oh, no," he whispered, as though horrified. He stopped as his legs hit his bed and she kept coming until she was pressed fully to his length. "That could take all night."

She smiled.

Crushing her in his embrace, playfulness turned to passion with the suddenness of a summer squall.

The force of their excitement drenched them, making their kisses slick with need, their hands trembling with the beat of their hearts.

Melodie became the center of his world, her body the only thing that existed. There was only the taste of her, like tasting rhythm; only the feel of her, like touching harmony; only the smell of her, like inhaling a symphony.

He vowed to himself and to her that he would love her until she was replete, and then he would love her more, filling her until there was no room for doubt.

And she gave to him as much as she took. She claimed the lead before he had even had a moment to catch his breath, and she flowed her love over him like a wave on the beach. She was warm and fluid and tasted of salt. She rose with her passion and crashed against him with her release.

The night watched as they danced.

And sang when they slept.

Morning came, as mornings do. But this time there was no tension, no confusion. Only a renewing of the evening's events that this time included laughter, playfulness and teasing.

"So you and your folks talked, huh?" he asked, kissing her forehead when they finally edged apart.

"Yeah. Everything's not perfect, but I think we've made a small start."

"I'm glad."

"Me, too. I never thought...I mean, I'd hoped for a long time but never really expected this to happen."

The silence between them was comfortable. Trent traced lazy patterns down her back as she rested on his chest.

"You know," she murmured as she raised her head and wiped at the sheen of perspiration on his lip, "we've never said the words."

That suspicious jerking motion at the corner of his mouth was back. "What words are those?"

She punched him in the stomach.

He gave an exaggerated grunt and twisted, pulling her under him in one smooth motion, covering her completely. "Do you mean these words?" he asked, using kisses as punctuation. "I . . . love . . . you, Melodie Allford. More than anything I have ever loved or will love again."

She smiled.

And waited.

His expression turned mockingly serious. "Your turn," he prompted.

She broke down. "I love you, Trent. I love you, I love you, I love you."

"Then you'll marry me?"

"Ohh, I don't know. If I do, you might go all stodgy on me again."

"When was I ever stodgy?" he demanded, rolling off of her and sitting on the edge of the bed. "I'm not stodgy."

She slithered over and laid her head on his thigh. "Oh, I don't know. There was a time when one Trenton James Laroquette, the Third, was quite put off by a certain redhead in a tie-dyed shirt and piggy leggings."

"I wasn't put off, I was just . . . surprised."

"Uh-huh. And just where was I on your list? Come on, be honest."

"You were never on any list," he answered honestly.

"See? I told you."

He rolled her on her back again and loomed over her. "You weren't on any list because you are one of a kind. And you're *my* one of a kind."

Apparently her underlying concern was not as well hidden as she'd thought, for Trent's features lost all their frivolous humor and turned serious.

"What is it, sweetheart? I suddenly feel as if you're only half here."

She snorted in disgust and moved back to sit up against the headboard. "Let's get something straight right now. You do not have permission to read me like a book, is that understood?"

He chuckled dutifully, and reached over to trace a tender finger around the curve of her jaw. "I'll try. But since I'm already in the dog house this morning, do you want to enlighten me as to what's got you worked up all of a sudden?"

She dropped her eyes, as uncertain and afraid now as she'd been confident and passionate a few moments before.

"I'm not sure I can be a good wife, Trent."

"What? Melodie, that's—"

"Please don't say "silly." I'm deadly serious. I don't know if I can fit into your world."

"My world?" he asked, puzzlement etching furrows in his forehead.

She gave an exasperated sigh. "Trent, I don't know a pâté knife from a butter knife. I can hostess a pizza party, but not a seven-course meal."

When he burst out laughing, she felt a flush start at about the base of her ankles and spread all the way up.

Trent sprawled across her thighs, propping his elbow on a pillow and his head on his hand. "This may come as a shock to you, but I'm hardly a member of Austin's social elite."

"Oh, really? So who was that man dressed to kill in a custom-fit tuxedo and going to a charity gala? Your average Joe doesn't go to affairs like that."

"What does that have to do with anything? I went to represent the firm."

"Which you own most of."

Trent sat up and looked at her with a mixture of confusion and frustration. "Melodie, what's your point? So my firm is involved in some philanthropic causes. What does that have to do with us?"

Tears formed in Melodie's eyes. "Don't you see? You and I are from two different worlds. I can't mix and mingle with the kind of people you do. I'll stick out like a sore thumb."

He caught a tear as it fell down her cheek. "This is really bothering you, isn't it? I . . . I just can't believe you're so worried."

Melodie wound a strand of hair around her finger. "Of course I'm worried. What are you going to do the first time you need me to appear on your arm at some function, and I can't because I've got a recital?"

"I'll go alone."

She sniffed and reached to the night stand for a tissue. "Oh, sure, you say that now. But when it really happens, you'll get angry with me for not putting you first."

Trent looked at her for a long time before he sighed. "So that's what this is really about. You think I want to change you."

"Not now, maybe. For the moment I'm an interesting diversion. But when I start interfacing with your career, things will be different."

With an even deeper sigh, he sat up and hauled her into his arms before resettling them on the bed. He wanted to hold her while he looked deeply into her eyes.

"Melodie," he began, kissing her temple, "let me explain something. I want you to listen because I'm not going to let this tear you up. I didn't start out wealthy. I made my fortune by doing things my way and defying all the people who said I couldn't. I am not about to start jumping through other people's hoops at this late stage."

"But—"

"No buts. I love you and I want you to be my wife. I love your quirky sense of humor, I love your independence, I love the way you drive me wild in bed. The list is endless. And nowhere on that list is a line for changing you."

Relief flooded through her, but some doubt still remained.

"So you'll love me even if I accidentally use a soup spoon to stir my tea?"

"It'll be tough, but even then."

"Even if I don't wear white to our wedding?"

She waited, holding her breath as he stretched to pull her head over for a kiss.

"Especially then...."

Trenton paced the vestibule of the church, the tails of his pearl gray tuxedo flapping out behind him as he executed each turn. His best friend since college stood relaxed, leaning against a marble wall. Glen stood beside him, and Trenton wanted to strangle the two of them as they watched him twitch.

Any minute now they would head up to the altar to wait for the blushing bride and her attendants. And wait. And wait.

He wondered if it was uncommon for a groom to pass out.

Women did this on purpose, he decided. This was some kind of test, some rite of passage. Well, he wasn't going to put up with it! He was going to—

March right up to the altar like a good boy and wait.

Lord above, what was she going to do to him? She and Bridgette had twittered like schoolgirls as they'd planned and schemed. Oh, they'd called him when they'd needed him. Stand here, Trent. Sit here, Trent. Pay for this, Trent. Order boutonnieres, Trent. Don't forget gifts for the groomsmen, Trent.

He might as well have been ten years old again for all the credit they gave him. And he'd die before telling them he'd been at the jeweler's at nine o'clock this morning, in his tux, asking the nice lady what a guy gave to groomsmen. He hoped they liked the money clips....

He and the other two Stooges made their entrance at the scheduled time, and he stood there, a mild smile pasted on his mouth as his brain whirled.

She was enjoying this. He just knew it. She'd planned all along to leave him here, wondering if she was going to pop into the entryway down at the end of that aisle in some out-of-this-universe creation of purple and puce. At least, if she was going to wear something like that, she could have let him wear jeans and flip-flops so they'd match. But nooooo, *he* was the one who was going to look like a dope.

The only thing that relaxed him in the slightest was the sight of Amber, walking down the aisle in her violet dress, satin swishing over her petticoats. She carefully threw her rose petals from her white basket like the angel she was.

Joey looked quite the little man in his miniature tuxedo. He carried the ring pillow as though it might bite him.

And there was Bridgette, smiling prettily as she made her way next. Then Melodie's best girlfriend, Serena.

He watched the empty doorway, sweat forming on his forehead, his throat tightening. He saw Melodie's father, carefully making his way to his place, and then—

He saw her. And time stopped. At least his heart did.

Never, as God was his witness, had he ever seen anything more incredibly, breathtakingly beautiful than the vision who stepped beside her father and settled the train of her ivory satin gown behind her.

As she walked slowly toward him, their eyes locked, Trenton forced down the voice in his mind that said, "Just wait. The day's not over."

Through the ceremony, he could not take his eyes off the creation who was agreeing to be his wife for richer and poorer, for better and worse....

She was too beautiful. She deserved better than him. She deserved a prince on a white charger and a castle and swans on a lake....

But she was smiling at him, and saying, "I do," and blushing as he slid his ring onto her finger.

Then she was tugging him down the aisle, laughing her sweet laugh, and it was too late. She was stuck with him.

He didn't remember pictures. They must have done pictures because all of a sudden he was having a piece of cake smashed into his mouth. Melodie was laughing again.

She threw the bouquet and everyone was clapping.

And the voice came back.

As he slid the yards of ivory satin up Melodie's equally satiny leg, he heard laughter around him, but it sounded as if he were suddenly in a well. And then he saw it. And something snapped, and he started laughing. And laughing. And laughing.

He stopped his task long enough to straighten and pull her to him to kiss the ever-living daylights out of her. Then he bent again and removed the dainty, lace-trimmed, tie-dyed garter from above her knee.

He made sure Glen caught it.

* * * * *

Made in MONTANA

by Jackie Merritt

The Fanon family—born and raised in
Big Sky Country...and heading for a wedding!

Meet them in these books from
Silhouette Special Edition® and
Silhouette Desire® beginning with:

MONTANA FEVER
Desire #1014, July 1996

MONTANA PASSION
That Special Woman!
Special Edition #1051, September 1996

And look for more MADE IN MONTANA titles
in 1996 and 1997!

Don't miss these stories of ranching and love
only from Silhouette Books!

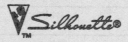

Take 4 bestselling love stories FREE

Plus get a FREE surprise gift!

'Tis the season for holiday weddings!

This December, celebrate the holidays
with two sparkling new love stories—
only from

SILHOUETTE YOURS TRULY™

A Nice Girl Like You
by Alexandra Sellers

Sara Diamond may be a nice girl, but that doesn't mean
she wants to be Ben Harris's ideal bride. But she might
just be able to play Ms. Wrong long enough to help this
confirmed bachelor find his true wife! That is, if she
doesn't fall in love first....

A Marry-Me Christmas
by Jo Ann Algermissen

All Catherine Jordan wanted for Christmas was some
time away from the hustle and bustle. Now she was
sharing a wilderness cabin with her infuriating opposite,
Stone Scofield! But once she stood under the mistletoe
with Stone, she was hoping for a whole lot more
this holiday....

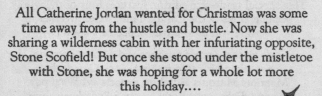

 Don't miss these exciting new books,
our gift to you this holiday season!

Look us up on-line at: http://www.romance.net

XMASYT

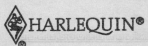 

SILHOUETTE... Where Passion Lives

Order these Silhouette favorites today!
Now you can receive a discount by ordering two or more titles!

SD#05890	TWO HEARTS, SLIGHTLY USED	
	by Dixie Browning	$2.99 U.S. ☐ /$3.50 CAN. ☐
SD#05899	DARK INTENTIONS	
	by Carole Buck	$2.99 U.S. ☐ /$3.50 CAN. ☐
IM#07604	FUGITIVE FATHER	
	by Carla Cassidy	$3.50 U.S. ☐ /$3.99 CAN. ☐
IM#07673	THE LONER	
	by Linda Turner	$3.75 U.S. ☐ /$4.25 CAN ☐
SSE#09934	THE ADVENTURER	
	by Diana Whitney	$3.50 U.S. ☐ /$3.99 CAN. ☐
SSE#09867	WHEN STARS COLLIDE	
	by Patricia Coughlin	$3.50 U.S. ☐
SR#19079	THIS MAN AND THIS WOMAN	
	by Lucy Gordon	$2.99 U.S. ☐ /$3.50 CAN. ☐
SR#19060	FATHER IN THE MIDDLE	
	by Phyllis Halldorson	$2.99 U.S. ☐ /$3.50 CAN. ☐
YT#52001	WANTED: PERFECT PARTNER	
	by Debbie Macomber	$3.50 U.S. ☐ /$3.99 CAN. ☐
YT#52008	HUSBANDS DON'T GROW ON TREES	
	by Kasey Michaels	$3.50 U.S. ☐ /$3.99 CAN. ☐
	(Limited quantities available on certain titles.)	

TOTAL AMOUNT	$ _____
DEDUCT: 10% DISCOUNT FOR 2+ BOOKS	$ _____
POSTAGE & HANDLING	$ _____
($1.00 for one book, 50¢ for each additional)	
APPLICABLE TAXES*	$ _____
TOTAL PAYABLE	$ _____
(check or money order—please do not send cash)	

To order, complete this form and send it, along with a check or money order for the total above, payable to Silhouette Books, to: **In the U.S.:** 3010 Walden Avenue, P.O. Box 9077, Buffalo, NY 14269-9077; **In Canada:** P.O. Box 636, Fort Erie, Ontario, L2A 5X3.

Name: _____

Address: _____ City: _____

State/Prov.: _____ Zip/Postal Code: _____

*New York residents remit applicable sales taxes.
 Canadian residents remit applicable GST and provincial taxes.

SBACK-SN3

Ⓥ Silhouette®
™

As seen on TV!
Free Gift Offer

With a Free Gift proof-of-purchase from any Silhouette® book, you can receive a beautiful cubic zirconia pendant.

This gorgeous marquise-shaped stone is a genuine cubic zirconia—accented by an 18" gold tone necklace.

(Approximate retail value $19.95)

Send for yours today...
compliments of ▼ *Silhouette*®
™

To receive your free gift, a cubic zirconia pendant, send us one original proof-of-purchase, photocopies not accepted, from the back of any Silhouette Romance™, Silhouette Desire®, Silhouette Special Edition®, Silhouette Intimate Moments® or Silhouette Yours Truly™ title available in August, September, October, November and December at your favorite retail outlet, together with the Free Gift Certificate, plus a check or money order for $1.65 U.S./$2.15 CAN. (do not send cash) to cover postage and handling, payable to Silhouette Free Gift Offer. We will send you the specified gift. Allow 6 to 8 weeks for delivery. Offer good until December 31, 1996 or while quantities last. Offer valid in the U.S. and Canada only.

Free Gift Certificate

Name: _____

Address: _____

City: _____ State/Province: _____ Zip/Postal Code: _____

Mail this certificate, one proof-of-purchase and a check or money order for postage and handling to: SILHOUETTE FREE GIFT OFFER 1996. In the U.S.: 3010 Walden Avenue, P.O. Box 9077, Buffalo NY 14269-9077. In Canada: P.O. Box 613, Fort Erie, Ontario L2Z 5X3.

FREE GIFT OFFER   084-KMD
ONE PROOF-OF-PURCHASE
To collect your fabulous FREE GIFT, a cubic zirconia pendant, you must include this original proof-of-purchase for each gift with the properly completed Free Gift Certificate.

084-KMD-R

The spirit of the holidays...
The magic of romance...
They both come together in

You're invited as Merline Lovelace and Carole Buck—
two of your favorite authors from two of your favorite
lines—capture your hearts with five joyous love stories
celebrating the excitement that happens when you
combine holidays and weddings!

Beginning in October, watch for

HALLOWEEN HONEYMOON by Merline Lovelace
(Desire #1030, 10/96)

Thanksgiving—
WRONG BRIDE, RIGHT GROOM by Merline Lovelace
(Desire #1037, 11/96)

Christmas—
A BRIDE FOR SAINT NICK by Carole Buck
(Intimate Moments #752, 12/96)

New Year's Day—
RESOLVED TO (RE)MARRY by Carole Buck
(Desire #1049, 1/97)

Valentine's Day—
THE 14TH...AND FOREVER by Merline Lovelace
(Intimate Moments #764, 2/97)

You're About to Become a
Privileged Woman

Reap the rewards of fabulous free gifts and benefits with proofs-of-purchase from Silhouette and Harlequin books

Pages & Privileges™

It's our way of thanking you for buying our books at your favorite retail stores.

PROOF OF PURCHASE
SD-PP19

Offer expires March 31, 1997

Harlequin and Silhouette—
the most privileged readers in the world!

For more information about Harlequin and Silhouette's PAGES & PRIVILEGES program call the Pages & Privileges Benefits Desk: 1-503-794-2499

SD-PP19